CW01507443

This book is dedicated to my late Grandma.

Also, thanks to my wife, for being patient and so forgiving as I never actually told her I was writing this until near the end.

Also, thank you to all my beta readers. I couldn't have done this without you guys.

Contents

Prologue

I take in a deep breath and open my chestnut brown eyes. Confusion and disorientation are the buzz words, it takes me a few moments to notice my surroundings and my current predicament. I am tied crucifix style, to a grey breeze block wall with chains.

I attempt to struggle out of the chains, but all of my strength has left me. I quickly give up. I survey the concrete room I am in. Dimly lit by one fluorescent strip. The only furnishing is a simple wooden table in the far corner. On top of the table, there are various grim-looking instruments—a steak knife, a machete, an assault rifle, and what looks like dynamite.

The only other thing in the room is a vast landscape mirror opposite me.

I was draped in a white hospital gown, Not pleased about this I stare at my pasty toned physique in the mirror. I see a shadow move behind it, and realise it is a one-way window.

"Hello," I call in a hoarse voice that I don't recognise. "Is anyone there?"

A moment later, the door to the room opens and in walks a tall person in black combat gear and wearing a black balaclava over his face.

"Hey mate, let me out of this."

He ignores me, "Hello? The least you can do is tell me where I am." Without a word, he crosses the room to the table.

He looks down and picks up the steak knife. My stomach sinks. Before turning back to me, he throws a cursory glance into the window mirror.

Instantaneously, I notice above the one-way window, a speaker. As if on cue, a deep male voice comes through on a speaker. "Proceed with test one."

"What's test one?" I ask, getting increasingly anxious as the balaclava-wearing man advances on me.

The man stops inches away from my face. Even through the balaclava I can smell his breath, which faintly reminds me of spaghetti bolognaise.

It is easy to understand what this man is about to do. Panic starts boiling inside me.

I beg the man, "Uh hey, you want to reconsider what you're gonna do? I'd really appreciate it."

Showing no emotion, the man plunges the steak knife all the way to the hilt into my chest just where my heart is. For a moment, the coldness of the blade going in is accentuated by the coppery taste on my tongue. I don't have time to process the pain. I instantly die.

I'm not aware of how much time has passed but eventually, I take in a deep breath and open my eyes again. I look down. The wound has healed. Lately, dying has become second nature for me. The man is standing in front of me.

"How long was I dead?"

No answer.

In the time it has taken me to heal and come back, he has replaced the knife with the assault rifle.

I imagine he took his time as methodically as a kid at a candy shop would.

He lifts the gun until the barrel is pointing straight at my head. My eyes cross trying to focus on the end. All I can see is a big black hole.

"Proceed with test two," the emotionless voice over the speakers demands.

Before I have time to react, I hear him squeeze the trigger, firing one shot, point-blank.

I imagine blood and grey brain matter splashing on the wall like a large rock into a small pond, If the movies and tv shows on the tele are right, it will drop to the floor, with a few droplets splattering back over the man's balaclava. I've seen too many movies, shows, and documentaries to know the damage a weapon like this could do at this range. There is a golf ball-sized hole in the middle of my forehead that you can see right through to the other side.

My head flops listlessly to the side. I don't have time to process anything as my world instantly becomes black, again.

Again an unknown amount of time passed before I open my eyes once the wound has healed.

It must have only been mere moments as the man is patiently waiting with the assault rifle still.

Once awake, the man goes back one step and sets the assault rifle to full-on automatic aiming for my chest.

"No, please wait," I plead feebly, close to tears and exhaustion. Dying, I learn is painful both physical and psychological. It plays havoc with my self-esteem.

Once again, ignoring me, the man squeezes the trigger raining a hail of bullets into my chest and stomach.

In the small confined space of the room, the sound of the gun firing is just a loud, offensive cacophony of noise that reverberates off the walls and my ears. The noise doesn't seem to affect my torturer as he just stands there calmly firing at me. His eyes are blank.

I feel the first half dozen bullets piercing my body. Before I die again, I remember it's like I am being struck in the chest by thousands of sharp stones. My body flails about like a rag doll in a vicious dog's mouth as the man shoots an entire clip of bullets into me.

I am long dead before the clip runs out. I imagine when it does my body resembles a bloody slice of swiss cheese with hundreds of bullet holes covering my entire torso and stomach.

This time as I am coming to, I could hear my torturer talking to somebody behind the window.

"The healing process seems to take longer this time." He is saying, "It seems to be dependent on the level of trauma."

The man has a slight cockney accent that sounds familiar.

"Who are you?" I ask wearily.

The man spins around and starts towards me. Instead of a rifle, he is now holding a machete.

"Who are you?" I repeat with what I hope is more force. "I recognise your voice."

"You should. We were at Cairo Airport when we last met."

I realise and remember who he is a split second before he pulls his mask off..

Eyes wide, "You," I say with a mix of fear, confusion, and anger."Why are you doing this to me?"

Before Sean can answer, the voice over the speakers cuts him off. "Proceed with test three."

Wordlessly, with a cold smirk, Sean raises the machete and slashes my body countless times. I scream, but he doesn't care. He plunges the cold weapon into me, over and over again, that sadistic smile never leaves his face.

I imagine the screams and the squelchy chopping sounds being heard outside the room, if there is anyone who cares enough to listen to them, are either sickly entertaining or informative.

After a few moments, the screams and chopping sound silence.

*

I'm not sure how long I have been in this room for. I lose count of the times they find increasingly inventive ways to kill me but it must be a fair few weeks judging by my beard growth.

I learn to mark the days passing by the occasional extended periods that Sean or some other person wearing a balaclava leave me on my own.

On a few occasions, my torturers will leave a bomb in the room and run out before it explodes. Each time the yield gets stronger. Each time I get blown into lots of little pieces. And each time I wake up out of my chains on the cold concrete floor. I am usually naked.

On one such occasion, I am sitting on the floor with my back to the wall and staring into nothingness. Over time, I have become a broken man. I have long gone past depression. I no longer cry or plead for help when my torturers come in. I have become desensitised towards my own death. Instead, I just stare into the middle distance waiting for the inevitable. I have actually forgotten who I am.

I am obviously going crazy. Hallucinations are proof of this. For example the mouse that keeps finding its way into my room. It will tell me what the weather is like outside and then leave.

So when a man I do not recognise suddenly appears in front of me without opening the door to the room first and coming through I naturally think I am having one such hallucination.

"Hello." The man says. He is sitting crossed legged facing me. He is dressed all in black with a leather hood over his head. From what I could see off his face he has a long grey beard and piercing eyes that look familiar. The ornate handle of a long sword held in a leather sheath with straps that criss cross his front is poking out from behind him.

When I don't initially respond he kicks my foot. *Can hallucinations touch you?*

"What do you want?" I ask wearily

"What do I want?" The man echoes, confused.

"Yes."

"The question is what do you want?"

"Who are you?"

"A friend."

"You know me?"

"Yes."

"Who am I? How did I get here?"

"Oh boy they have really done a number on you?" The man sympathises "Your name is Simon and how you got here is a long story."

"Can you tell me?"

"Of course. Sit back and for what it's worth try to get comfortable and I shall start from the beginning."

Chapter 1

On a bright spring sunny late morning, you hustled out of the exit of a fifteen-floor glass and concrete building in the middle of Canary Wharf.

When you felt like you got a safe distance, you stopped, slightly flushed, and out of breath. You looked back around, expecting someone to be following you out of the building.

"Did someone follow me?" I interrupt

"No." The bearded man says clearly put off by my interruption.

"What was I doing there?"

"All shall become clear. Can I continue?"

"Of course. Sorry, continue."

"Shit," You said to yourself, "I'm definitely not getting that job, you stupid, stupid…" Standing in the middle of the affluent Canary Wharf with hundreds of business types walking past and imposing skyscrapers climbing high. You looked like you were on the verge of a mass anxiety attack.

You swallowed hard. Thankfully, it didn't happen. Pulling yourself together by physically readjusting the lapels of your navy tailored fit suit, You proceeded to walk back to Green Park Underground Station to return home.

Walking, you retrieved your smartphone out of your trouser pocket and called Vasia.

"Vasia? She sounds familiar. Should I know her?

Clearly not liking the interruption again the man face palms.

"Sorry." I apologise

"Vasia is your wife." The man explains. "I promise all will become clear. Let me tell your story and if you have any questions ask at the end."

"Ok, I promise not to interrupt again."

"Thank you."

She interrupted before you could say "Hello", "So how did it go?"

You hesitated half a breath, "Well…"

"That bad was it?" Vasia asked sympathetically.

"It was a complete disaster, love."

"It couldn't have been that bad."

"Imagine the worst possible interview you have ever had."

There was only the sound of her breathing before she spoke again.

"Oh, God." Vasia groaned.

You couldn't help but grin. After fifteen years together, with ten of those married, you can sometimes tell precisely what she was thinking. She was probably remembering all the job interviews where old balding sweaty men leered at her boobs.

"Well, now that times a thousand," you emphasized.

"Babe! No! You know you're always down on yourself after one of these things. I bet you nailed it."

Her encouragement washed over you like a welcome hot shower.

"I told the idiot of an interviewer he was a joke."

"You didn't," she almost shouted.

"Imagine David Brent in The Office mixed with The Twilight Zone." You started telling her about your interview getting progressively stranger.

"What? He asked you why tennis balls are fluffy?" She cut off your description.

"Yup, and I've just googled it. That's what he's done to me, Vasia. He's made me google why tennis balls are fluffy. And do you know what I found?"

"What?" she hesitated.

"Nothing. Google doesn't even have an answer for it. And that wasn't even the worst question. He asked me whether or not I believe in ghosts."

"Oh, no. You didn't tell him, did you?" Vasia groaned.

As had been said before, you have been together for a really long time. So Vasia had a unique perspective on what questions and topics can make you go on a rant for ages. And ghosts are one of those things.

"Damn straight, I did. So when he pointed out on my CV, it says I'm outgoing and all that crap. He asked me to tell him a joke."

"And you said he was." Vasia finished, getting the picture.

You nodded in agreement as if Vasia could see that on the other end of the line.

"Oh, well." she sighed. "I guess there are other job interviews."

"Yes," you responded, "There will be."

"But you can't speak to people like that. If you want to get a job, you have to grin and bear it." Vasia lectured, and you rolled your eyes. "As my mum likes to say so eloquently, you have to be all tits and teeth."

"I know." Was all you could say.

The strain of being unemployed since the French-owned IT company went under during the most recent economic crisis was showing.

As you were nearing Green Park Station, Vasia changed the subject.

"How did your run go this morning? I was performing my Fajr and forgot to ask before you left the house."

Vasia was referring to her morning prayers and to your training for the London marathon.

"Yeah, it went well," you responded. "I ran eight miles in just under seventy minutes."

"Wow, that's good for you," Vasia said supportively.

She knew you and your goals and how badly you wanted to do this. That was one of the things you two appreciated about each other. Your drive to complete things.

"Yeah, I feel like training is coming on really nicely."

You were just going through the entrance of Green Park when Vasia asked: "How did the journey to London go?"

"It was uneventful, really," You answered, really selling it, "When I got to St Pancras though, I met these interesting people on the underground platform. Some tribal people from Africa; I think. Got talking to the grandfather and this pretty young lady with braids, I think their names were Eraaf and Ermee."

"Pretty was she?" Vasia immediately asked.

You could see her eyes smiling.

You laughed. "Not like that. You know I only have eyes for you."

"Well, when you say you meet pretty girls on the Underground, what else am I going to think?" She said.

She tried to sound serious, but you knew she was pulling your leg.

"Anyway." You carried on as you went through the turnstiles with your Oyster card, "Just had a pleasant conversation with them. Although the grandfather kept freaking me out. He kept staring and smiling at me. They call themselves the Xuholo tribe. They live somewhere called the Volta on the borders between Chad, Sudan, and Libya."

"That's nice," Vasia said, sounding ropey.

As you were travelling down the escalator, you put it down to the signal about to cut out.

"Listen, Vasia. I'm going down to the Underground, and my signal is about to cut out. I'll see you when I get home."

Faintly you could hear Vasia acknowledge with, ``See you later." when the phone suddenly cut out.

Shrugging you put your phone back in your pocket and proceeded down the busy escalator and to the platform.

Chapter 2

Halfway back from Canary Wharf to Green Park, you noticed the Xuholo tribe people that you had just been talking to Vasia about, were on the same train again. They were on the next carriage over.

The train was too overcrowded to move on, and you were slightly apprehensive about stepping from one carriage to the other on a moving train in a dark tunnel. You resorted to giving Ermee a nod and a smile through a scratched and grimy window when she noticed you.

At Westminster, the last stop before Green Park, you noticed a tall, muscular figure in a dark green hoodie with the hood pulled up stepping off. Before the doors whooshed shut, You saw that he had left a black canvas backpack on the seat he had been sitting in.

"Hey?" You shouted after the hooded man

The man froze in mid-step but did not turn around, at first.

"Your bag," You shouted again as the doors closed.

The figure turned. The hood obscured most of his face, so you couldn't make out any distinguishing features, but you had the uneasy feeling that the figure was grinning at you. The kind of smile used by the villain in almost every comic book and action movie.

Your uneasiness steadily grew as the train moved off again. Before it entered the tunnel and the figure disappeared from view, you saw the guy reaching into his pocket and retrieved a mobile phone.

Instinct told you that something was very wrong and that you were doing an incredibly dumb thing by stepping over to the backpack and looking inside. But that's precisely what you did!

What you saw caused the hairs on the back of your neck to stand on end.

Holding your breath, You took a minute to really take in what you were seeing. A black rectangular cylinder that took up most of the bag. It had various coloured wires connected to a see-through plastic container that contained a thick-looking liquid.

Having not been brought up in circles where bombs were commonplace, you wouldn't have known, but there was no mistaking that this was one.

As a sickening, dreadful feeling took hold of you, a red digital countdown timer suddenly appeared on the black box, and, with a little beep, it started counting down from ninety seconds. The thick substance changed colour when the timer started.

What happened next happened fast, yet to you, it felt like everything was in slow motion.

Turning to the rest of the people, you screamed like a banshee. "EVERYBODY MOVE THERE IS A BOMB"

At first, everybody stayed in their seats, staring at you gormlessly. Many were plugged into their electronics and no doubt didn't hear you. Some just thought you were mad.

"THERE IS A FUCKING BOMB YOU IDIOTS, MOVE!" You shouted again in frustration.

As soon as you mentioned the "b" word again, everyone got the idea and, as one unit, started screaming,

18

panicking. They stampeded to the other end of the carriage, crashing and shoving each other out of the way.

Just two metres in front of you, an eight-year-old Asian boy got trampled on in the mad rush, and you immediately stepped over to the boy to help him up. As you got the boy back on his feet, the mother, wearing a black Hajib, and who must have realised her son wasn't with her, doubled back and appeared running against the tide of people. She must not have understood your intentions as she took one look at you holding her son's hand, presumed the worst, and screamed in your face; her spittle flew into your face, and her breath smelled of cinnamon.

With surprising strength for her size, she shoved you to the floor. Barely stopping, she picked up her son and ran back after the mob of people.

Slightly stunned and shaken, more out of the sudden confrontation than getting hurt from the fall, you got back on your feet. You saw someone had got the door open to the next carriage. Giving no thought to their safety, and they were in a dark tunnel on a moving train, they were leaping from one carriage to the other. As everyone piled into that one, the original occupants also caught on and turned to flee the unknown horror.

Remembering that there was another carriage behind you, you turned around to see the people (including Ermee and her tribe) on that carriage just crowded around the windows peering in at you. For a moment, you had this weird feeling that they were like spectators watching fish in an aquarium.

However, realising that over the noise of the train, they could probably not hear my frantic shouts that there was a bomb, you ran back up the carriage taking a brief look in the backpack. For a moment, you casually wondered how only twenty seconds had gone past at this point.

With all your strength, you yanked the door open to the carriage, and, taking no heed to your previous apprehension, you jumped from one to the other.

Once in the other carriage, you started shepherding the occupants to the other end.

As soon as you mentioned the bomb again, everyone reacted as one and dashed to the other end, trying to budge off the carriage crashing into each other as they pushed and shoved.

That was all apart from the Xuholo tribe, who just stood together as one unit, looking with serious interest at you.

You frantically turned to Ermee, "Please get your people to the other end. Something bad will happen."

As if getting the message for the first time, Ermee turned to her people, said something in her mother tongue, and they too scattered up the carriage. Apart from Eraaf. A task in itself on a moving train, he was standing on one leg holding his wooden staff. He was staring at you with that same look he had when you two first met earlier that morning.

You had that slightly weirded out feeling again, especially when the tribal leader gave a half bow, turned, and strolled after the others as if he was on some leisurely walk through Clapham Common.

The bomb momentarily forgotten, you stared after the old man, half-dazed, but you were rudely dragged out of your trance when the intercom announced you were approaching Green Park.

Immediately you realised this bomb would explode at a packed station. As if you were running on some adrenaline-fuelled instinct you spun into action. Noticing the emergency brake on the wall; you pulled it with all your strength.

A horrible screeching noise and a hard jolt forced you headfirst into a pole in the middle of the floor with an audibly painful clang. You felt your head ricochet off the pole and for less than a second you wondered if you have whip-lash.

The train started its painfully slow process of stopping, but unfortunately, it would not stop soon enough.

Seeing stars, and feeling a bitter metallic taste in your mouth, you gained your balance before hitting the floor and, unmindful of the bloody wound that had just opened on your forehead, half stumbling you started running up the carriage.

You caught up to an elderly white-haired lady who had been rudely thrown to the floor when you had pulled the emergency brake.

You helped her back to her feet and supported her with one arm around her waist. The two of you ran as fast as she could muster. You headed up the carriage to where the other people were trying to get into the next car.

Just before you caught up with the others, everyone screamed as the lights went out. You and everyone else were plunged into total darkness if it wasn't for the metal wheels grating on metal tracks making sparks outside the train. This was causing an eerie strobe-like effect seen from inside the train. Your heart started racing and panic exploded through your whole body. Suddenly, you couldn't breathe.

Chapter 3

Your eyes blinked open. Your head was pounding, and your body disorientated as you realised you had woken up upside down. Your entire body was hanging in an odd angle that would make any yoga teacher proud. You knew you had to right yourself, but as you slowly moved your body, the pain caused your head to start spinning and you almost blackout again.

Falling to your hands and knees, You stayed stock still as you tried to shake off the fog that was clouding your head. Disorientated, nothing was computing. Nothing made sense. The only way you can describe the feeling is to liken it to a computer after it had rebooted. First, there's blackness, and slowly things come together.

Rather than hearing them, you slowly sensed the screams of dying and injured people. You looked to your left and then wished you hadn't. You recognised the old lady you had tried to save lying beside you. Dead. The yellow vertical grab rail poking out of her right eye socket was the biggest clue. Her head looked like it was detached from the rest of her body. It was just hanging on by the few vertebrae of her spine.

You couldn't help a watery sensation in your mouth. You swallowed hard and wished you hadn't. The acid scratching of the bile crawled up your throat. You turned your head in the opposite direction and vomited.

After a few moments, you wiped your mouth with the back of your sleeve. With your whole body shaking almost uncontrollably, you tried to get up.

Your head hit something hard.

"Mother fucker!"

Seeing stars, you rubbed the spot. You staggered to your feet, ducking to avoid the object and looked around. The only illumination came from the cracked and dirty windows.

You finally understood what was adding to your disorientation. You were standing on the ceiling in an upside-down carriage, resting at an uphill slant. The object you had hit when trying to stand up was the head-rest of a seat. You desperately looked around for anyone who needed help. You were alone in the carriage. The groans, screams, and yells for help you were hearing over the painful ringing in your ears were coming from behind you in the next carriage.

You looked at the door separating the two carriages, and you bent down to look through the broken window only to find blackness. A seemingly endless void.

Your first thought was to squeeze through the window to the next carriage, but you quickly fathomed the space was too small for you to fit. You had no idea what was on the other side, either.

Panic clawed at your throat, and your heart felt like it was beating out of your ribcage as you realised you were trapped in this dark steel tube. Would this become your coffin?

Taking a deep breath to keep the panic from overwhelming you. You hurriedly walked to the middle doors that opened to whatever was left of the tunnel. You gingerly stepped over the grab rails on the ceiling. Fumbling around the wall in the pitch black. You found the button to open the door and pressed it.

Nothing.

Apart from a hissing noise, like air escaping the hydraulics, nothing happened.

You pressed the button again.

Still nothing but the hissing noise and distant moans of those dying.

In frustration, you repeatedly banged on the button, getting the same result each time.

You had never felt so alone, so helpless.

"HELP." You yelled as you started banging on the doors.

You kept yelling until your throat hurt, and your voice went hoarse. Still nobody came.

"Calm down, Simon. Breathe." You tried to self-soothe.

You stopped banging on the door to catch your breath. You were just about to start again when someone behind you moaned in a strangled tone.

"Help."

The ghostly sound chilled your soul. You looked up and down in the darkness until your eyes landed on the door to the adjoining carriage. Assuming the sound was coming from there, you rushed back to it and started shouting through the letterbox size space.

No answer.

You looked desperately around your surroundings and caught sight of the red glass box with a small hammer inside. The sign beside the box with the writing upside down read, "In case of emergency break glass."

"Well, if ever there was an emergency, this would be it." You muttered out loud.

You went over to the box and kicked the glass out to get the hammer. Choosing one of the side windows, you bashed the little hammer against the corner of it, and the window shattered.

Getting down on all fours being mindful of all the glass, debris, and stones on the track, you crawled out of the side window.

Standing, you pointlessly brushed the dirt and glass off your ripped, dirty, and blood covered suit.

Like a bolt of blue lightning, a fleeting memory passed through your mind of that morning. Of getting dressed for the interview and obsessing over the colours you wanted to wear. As if all that fussing would make any difference.

Vasia will kill me when she sees the state of me.' and for the briefest of moments you wondered if dying here would have been preferable to what she was going to do to you.

Your carriage was still in the dark gloom of the tunnel with a small sliver of light coming from the only exit in sight, the platform, about fifty yards away.

From your vantage point, you could see the station platform was in absolute chaos, with train carriages piled into each other. The front end of the train had mounted the platform and punched through the wall beside the existing tunnel making an extra one. There was rubble, dust, and cables spitting electricity everywhere. From this distance, you could see people were lying dead underneath the rubble.

A few lucky survivors, if you could all be called that, were wandering aimlessly around the wreckage; their dirty, dusty faces a mask of vacant shock and dismay. Others awkwardly climbed out of the side windows of the broken train wreckage or had got the doors opened and jumped the four feet to safety of the ground. Through the debris you could see that one person had accidently landed on the 3rd rail and been instantly electrocuted. Their smoking body filled the air with the smell of burnt flesh and smoldering death. The wretched stench forced some people to vomit bringing new meaning to the word 'uncontrollable'.

You watched an elderly man, in a similarly ripped suit, clumsily climb over the lip of the window and fall to the platform floor, smashing his head against the ground. You were sure the old man must have died right away or at the very least knocked himself out. To your surprise, he slowly sat up and, using the side of the train as support, dragged himself to his feet. Once upright, he swayed and looked confused for a few moments, then staggered off towards safety. You were forced to admire his resilience.

The faint and distant siren sounds of the emergency services combined with the cries of despair, but you could not see any professional help or hope.

You didn't have time to let all that sink in. You walked down the tunnel towards the station platform, your feet crunching on the gravel, gingerly avoiding rubble and broken cables.

You got as far as the middle of the first carriage after yours when you heard knocking from inside.

With them at shoulder height, you stepped over to the sliding doors and put your ear to the metal.

You could just make out someone sobbing and another person moaning from inside.

Desperate, you banged on the door and shouted, "Is anybody there?!"

This instantly started up a chorus of bangs,yells, and cries for help from inside.

"Hang on, I will get you out," you promised, shouting through the door, probably sounding more optimistic than you felt.

This started up another chorus of thank you, Gods, and bless yous with one saying, "Please hurry, I think this person is dying. I don't know how long they have. She's bleeding badly."

"No pressure Simon," you said under your breath.

You put your hands in the gap of the middle of the sliding doors, and with all your strength, you tried pushing them open.

They wouldn't budge.

You tried a second time. Sweat started pouring down to reward your exertion.

The problem was the doors were too high, and you couldn't get enough leverage to pry them apart.

You gave up for a second.

"Was I a tad optimistic when I said I would help everybody get out?" You quietly wondered to yourself with a very heavy sigh.

Not knowing what you were doing, you aimlessly started looking around for something to help you get the doors open.

Then inspiration struck you.

You ran back up the train to your carriage, and with some apprehension, you gingerly crawled back in the way you had come out.

Back inside, averting your eyes from the dead lady, you went to another vertical grab rail sticking out of the floor and after a few kicks and pulls, you broke it out of its socket

With the metal pole in hand, and more comfortable with your mouse hole exit, you crawled out and ran back down to the doors of the next carriage.

You slipped one end of the bar into the gap between the two doors and using it as a crowbar; you tried to pry the doors apart.

At first, the doors wouldn't budge, but slowly and surely, the doors opened with an angry screeching sound. With a gap wide enough to poke your head through, you peered in to look inside.

What you saw horrified you more than seeing the dead lady. To this day, the memory still gives you nightmares.

Two dozen people, six lying unconscious on the floor.

You weren't sure if they were all dead but were reasonably confident some of them should be. Blood gushed from the head of the nearest man, forming a widening pool around his body. Another person half sprawled over a seat, one of their arms caught between the seat and the wall of the train, twisted unnaturally. The most gruesome was the man pinned to the wall of the train by a pole, his red glistening intestines twisting around it like a macabre christmas decoration.

This last person, you recognised as one of the Xuholo tribes-people.

You diverted your eyes from the ghastly sight and stared at the person sitting cross-legged directly in front of you on the opposite side.

It was Eraaf. He was calmly looking at you with that same haunting stare from earlier that gave you the slight willies.

After a few moments, Eraaf looked down at the body that he was cuddling with the head on his lap. It took awhile for you to realise that it was Ermee, and she was unconscious.

"Please get us out," Eraaf said in a heavily accented and broken English.

Looking at the dilemma, his voice was almost too calm. On paper, it sounded like a desperate plea, but with Eraaf as serene as ever, it was as if he was asking the time of day.

You stared transfixed at Eraaf for a second. The plea did not compute at first, maybe because it sounded so bucolic, not in context with the situation you were in.

Breaking the spell, a blonde woman in her late twenties appeared at the door.

In what you thought was the first stages of a panic attack, the woman echoed Eraaf's plea, but with more feeling, and started pushing at the left door to get it open a little wider. You did the same with the right-hand door, and soon the two of you got them open all the way.

Not bothering to wait any longer, the woman jumped to the floor. You barely got your hand under her elbow, stopping her from falling flat on her face.

Without so much as a 'thank you', she sprinted up the tunnel, climbed up the platform, and disappeared.

You helped four other people out of the carriage. The last being a bearded Sikh man.

Before he wandered off, you asked, "How about a bunk up?"

You wanted to help Eraaf and Ermee.

Once inside the carriage, you knelt beside the two tribes-people and took Ermee's pulse.

It was weak but steady.

You turned to Eraaf, "She's still alive, but we have to hurry."

Eraaf nodded in agreement, and he immediately stood up. You couldn't help but notice, remarkably, he didn't have a scratch on him.

The two of you carried Ermee to the door where you both climbed out.

You took Ermee's legs, and, with Eraaf taking her front half, you carried her up the track to the platform.

Just as you climbed up to the platform, you heard some frantic knocking and turned around.

Maybe half a dozen young school children were standing at the doors of one carriage, looking out at you. With pale dirt-streaked faces, some crying but all looked absolutely terrified. They were pleading to be rescued.

Horrified, you set Ermee's legs on the ground with Eraaf still holding her up under her armpits and was about to head to the children's carriage when Eraaf in an urgent tone suddenly said, "No."

Impatiently you looked back at Eraaf, who got hold of Ermee with one arm and pointed at something with the other.

Your gaze followed the direction Eraaf was pointing towards, and after a moment, you let out a breathless gasp.

Just to the left of the doors of the carriage, there were cables draped over it and hanging two feet from the ground. They writhed and coiled like angry snakes as electricity sparked angrily from them.

This wasn't the most horrifying thing that caught your attention. It was the trail of oil coming from the front of the train and making its way slowly to the cables.

Chapter 4

Desperately you looked back at Eraaf who, despite the situation, still looked calm, shrugged his shoulders almost nonchalantly.

You starred in silent panic as you looked at the scared faces of the children, an unknown terror creeping towards them.

Finally, you decided. You stepped up to the carriage doors and shouted through them to the children a promise, "Hang on in there, I will be back."

Then you turned around and hurried back to where Eraaf and Ermee were.

You felt as if your heart was being ripped out of your chest. It took all your willpower to not turn back around when the children started screaming for help again.

Grabbing Ermee's legs, you grimly said to Eraaf, "I'll help you get Ermee out, and then I'm coming back."

Eraaf nodded his thanks, and the two of you carried Ermee, gingerly stepping around or over rubble and trying to avoid rebar.

On your way to the exit, you had a better view of the debris. You saw more of the dead bodies underneath and around them.

You had to divert your eyes when you saw a man. Well you presume he was a man. His decapitated head was some-place else, and a little girl with blood splattered all over her was lying motionless by his side. You surmise that this was his daughter.

You got to the exit. Debris blocked it, but seeing that the firefighters would be through soon, you left the two tribes-people and rushed back to the trapped children.

You pick up a piece of rebar on the way, and as soon as you got to the carriage doors, you slipped one end through the gap and, with grim determination, you set about getting the doors open, trying to ignore how close the trail of oil was getting to the electric cables.

The cheers and cries from the children gave you the motivation needed.

You got the doors open wide enough for one child, a six-year-old girl with blood in her blond pigtails, to slip a hand through the gap.

Despite the immediate and impending situation that you were all in, you stopped what you were doing for a moment to hold her hand

"Please get me out." she pleaded, ripping your heartstrings, "Miss Milton is asleep, and she won't wake up," the girl continued through sobs.

You weren't sure who Miss Milton was, but given the current situation, you hazarded a guess she most definitely was not taking a little cat nap.

"What's your name?" you asked the little girl trying to distract both of you.

"Jessica," she answered shyly.

With a calmness that you surely did not feel and a smile so phony it felt alien on your face, you reassured, "Jessica, I promise I will get you and your friends out."

Reluctantly, you let go of the girl's hand and with every ounce of strength you had, you opened the doors just barely wide enough to get the children out.

A faint whooshing sound joined the soft sobs of the children. Warmth spread up from your feet across your legs, causing your skin to heat. With a growing sense of fear, you glanced at the angry electrical cables. Dread engulfed your, the heat of the fire was now working its way along the trail left by the oil.

There must have been a moment when you contemplated turning around and hightailing it out of there. Instead:

"Ok," you said as you looked back at the children, trying to keep your voice as calm as possible "Let's play a game, shall we?"

"What's the game called?" Jessica asked her interest piqued.

"It's called get out of the train and run."

You must admit it needed a catchier title but not bad considering it was on the hoof.

"I like that game," Jessica said as you lifted her out first and set her on the ground.

You pointed towards the exit where you noticed the firefighters had got through the debris, and three of them were heading in their direction.

Jessica ran towards the firefighters. One of them took her by the hand and rushed her to the exit.

The other two helped carry the other children out of the carriage, and once all six of them were off, the two firefighters started herding the children towards the exit.

They probably got halfway there when they realised you weren't with them.

Once all the children were safely out of the carriage, you looked inside and saw there were more people inside. All were unconscious, but some looked like they were breathing.

Ignoring not only the fact that the carriage was catching fire you crushed your sense of self-preservation to run. You climbed into the carriage and quickly made your way up the carriage checking the bodies.

The first one you came across was a thirty-something brunette female. You had no reason to think this, but you guessed that this must be the teacher, the little girl Jessica referred to as Miss Milton.

She was unconscious with a deep cut in the crown of her head, forming a small pool of blood around her.

You checked her pulse and somehow found one, albeit it was faint.

The two firefighters sprinted back to the carriage.

One shouted, "Hey mister, get the hell out of there! The train is about to blow!"

"Why are you stating the obvious?" You wondered while ignoring them.

You carefully picked the lady up and carried her to the door where the firefighters took her.

They gave you a look that questioned your own desire to live. Quite honestly, it was something that kept screaming in your head. Through their turn out gear you could easily tell that one of them was a woman and the other a male. Both looked burly in their fall kit. They took the unconscious female. The male firefighter lifted her over his shoulders in a typical fireman's lift and carried her to safety. With him off, his partner stayed behind

"You have to get out!" she yelled trying to get you to leave.

You pretended to not hear her.

Unmindful of the flames lapping at the windows outside, you turned to search for more survivors. There had to be more than some children and an unconscious woman.

"There just has to be." You muttered loud enough that only you could hear your words.

You had reached the far end of the carriage when you saw the Asian lady sitting on the floor spread legged with her back against the dividing door to the other carriage. One of the vertical grab rails had detached itself from the floor and poked through the stomach, pinning her to the door.

Despite the gruesome sight, what caught your eye was the three-month-old baby boy lying in the crook of her arm. He was sucking on his dummy and calmly staring at you as you approached.

"He's not making any noise."

The scene with this baby was so surreal that you tuned out any and all sounds. You knelt by the woman, looking at the child. The woman's head was down with her chin touching her chest, and her eyes were closed. You were sure she was dead. So she scared the piss out of you when her eyes fluttered open and lifted her head to look you in the eyes. She smiled tiredly.

You smiled back with what you thought was calm friendliness

A tap on the shoulder reminded you that you weren't alone and it pulled you back to the reality at hand. You looked up to see the female firefighter standing there.

"Sir, we have to go now; it's not safe for you," the firefighter declared.

You finally had to admit that there was nothing else you could do for this woman or anyone else in the carriage.

"Ok, help me with this woman and child first."

The dying mother said, weakly but audibly, "Please save my baby."

The firefighter took a knee and leaned over to get a better look at the rail going through the lady's stomach.

She saw it went straight through, coming out of the bottom of her back and had embedded itself into the floor.

You noticed the look that expressed both hopelessness and understanding momentarily flash across the firefighter's face before professionalism took over. It didn't matter, your stomach had already dropped out of your body. She hid it well, probably from years of practice being in disastrous situations.

The firefighter knelt back on her haunches and looked at the lady square in the face.

"Madam, what is your name?"

"Khusbakht," the woman replied.

"Khusbakht," the firefighter repeated. "That is a beautiful name."

"It means lucky," Khusbakht said, smiling tiredly.

Ignoring the irony, the firefighter ploughed on.

"Khusbakht, I need you to understand the situation we are in," she started and then took a deep breath, "The whole train is primed to explode any second now. A fire has started outside. You can probably see it at the windows. You have a metal pole sticking out of your stomach, and it goes right through the bottom of your back, where you are losing quite a lot of blood. I don't have the equipment with me to remove it. I need to walk back to my fire engine to get it. If I do that, I don't have time to save you."

Before the firefighter could continue, the woman shook her head sadly but still smiling tiredly.

"Don't worry about me. Please save my baby?"

This was unfortunate and understanding what would happen next, you mournfully hung your head. However, the firefighter, ensuring she kept eye contact with the Asian woman, nodded her understanding, and reached for the baby. Khusbakht handed him gladly but with tears streaming from her eyes.

At that point, several of the windows exploded and shattered from the heat and fire. The firefighter and you jumped, and a look of panic spread across Khusbakht's face. How she managed to say the next part still haunts you.

"Go, go, go save my baby," she screamed.

The firefighter, remaining calm, asked "What's his name?"

"Shaquil." The mother answered smiling proudly.

"Do you have any next of kin? Does he have a father?"

"Yes."

Khusbakht gave the firefighter her husband's details before she repeated her last plea to save her baby.

With one last sad look at the Asian lady, the firefighter, carrying the baby, and you rushed to the doors of the carriage. You jumped off first and turned to take the baby from the firefighter, allowing her to get out.

Flames almost engulfed the outside of the carriage, and seconds after the firefighter jumped off, the fire engulfed the entrance, striking off any idea to go back inside.

The firefighter took the baby from you, and you ran towards the exit, which was now clear enough to allow people to get through.

The firefighter yelled, "Everyone get back! The train's gonna explode!"

Just as you got to the exit, you stopped and paused.

"Wait a second," you mumbled to anyone that was listening.

You were having second thoughts about leaving the lady behind.

You turned around and made to go back.

You managed two steps when your entire world went black.

The entire station shook as the front end of the train exploded into a mushroom cloud of flames. A chain reaction triggered similar explosions going up the line of carriages.

The ceiling caved in, exposing the London streets above.

For the briefest of moments, you remember the sun burning your eyes.

Before you lose consciousness, you remember the wave of intense heat, throwing you backward like a rag doll against the wall. You barely registered the pain as a sizable chunk of the ceiling knocked you out cold.

Chapter 5

The doors to St. Thomas Hospital slammed open, allowing two paramedics with a body on a gurney to sprint in.

The body on the gurney was you.

You had a deep gash down the left side of your head from the falling debris.

You were slipping in and out of consciousness, and to this day, you can only remember fragments here and there. You were wheeled straight into the operating theatre, and the doctors started preparing you for surgery.

In one lucid moment, you briefly opened your eyes and mumbled something.

A nurse standing closer to you bent down with her ear near your mouth and asked you to repeat, but the nurse could only make out one word.

"Vasia?" the nurse repeated. "Is that your wife?"

You vaguely remember nodding your head feeling like it weighed a ton.

"How do we get hold of her?" the nurse asked.

"Phone. Pocket" was all the nurse could make out.

However, and you did not know this at the time, but your phone was not in your pocket. One of the medical staff had already taken all your valuables and had put them in a plastic bag. This the nurse quickly located, pulled the phone out, and walked back to where you were lying on the operating table.

"I need to put a pin in to open it," the nurse explained. "What is it?"

"My name in numbers," you croaked cryptically.

You closed your eyes and lost consciousness for a few moments, leaving the nurse to ponder over the pin.

Your eyes fluttered open for a brief second, and you remember seeing a moment of inspiration fall on the nurse's face.

Before the doctors put a mask over your face for the anesthesia to start the operation, you saw the nurse walk out of the theatre with your phone to her ear. Presuming the nurse was calling Vasia you felt slight relief just before the drugs took over and you descended into blackness.

Chapter 6

Worried and flustered, a couple of minutes shy of an hour after the phone call, Vasia came running into the hospital. She practically barged her way into the operating theatre you were in.

She only got as far as the entranceway when a beefy looking security guard put a bone crushing hand on her shoulder and stopped her dead in her tracks.

A group of medical staff were gathered around a body on an operating table. One of the staff dressed all in scrubs complete with a surgical mask and face shield looked up from what he was doing and shouted. "How the hell did she get in here?"

"Sorry Doc," the security guard apologised

"I mean there are several security doors to get through. Literally how the fuck did she get in?" The doctor said with barely contained contempt..

"The lady was determined and a cleaner had propped up one of the doors while they were cleaning." The security guard explained.

"Well get her out of here! Someone check to make sure she didn't contaminate the room." The doctor demanded.

While this conversation was going on, Vasia desperately looked around the room and got a good look at the person on the operating table.

"Simon." She barely whispered.

The doctors had peeled back the skin on top of your head, taken away part of your skull, and were operating on your brain.

Vasia felt sick and had to put her hand out to steady herself before she almost fainted. She would have surely collapsed if the security guard wasn't holding her up.

As the doctor made his demands, the guard guided Vasia out to the corridor where a nurse, a kindly looking female in her fifties took over and guided her to some seats nearby.

"What's wrong with him?" She asked the nurse frantically.

"Your partner,,," the nurse started.

"My husband," Vasia corrected rather too defensively, "He's my husband. His name is Simon."

She was trying to slow down her rapid shallow breaths to stop herself from hyperventilating, or worse, fainting.

"Sorry, Mrs. Emerson."

"Call me, Vasia." She interrupted again.

The nurse was almost too patient and must have done this too many times to remember.

"Vasia." she corrected "Your husband is in a critical but in very stable condition. He is otherwise fit, healthy, and we expect him to recover."

"What's wrong with him?"

It almost came out like a cry of anguish.

The nurse sat down next to her and continued in patient, soothing tones.

"Simon is in the most capable hands in the country and, although, in a severe condition, they expect him to make a full recovery. He's very lucky that the doctor and his staff were in residence today. He has cuts and lacerations and is suffering from what they called an Acute subdural haematoma. In layman's terms, there is a blood clot putting pressure on his brain. He was very close to having an aneurysm. A stroke."

The horror on Vasia's face must have told her everything. The nurse carried on explaining to her that the doctors were currently performing a Craniotomy. This was a procedure where the doctors cut away a bit of the skull so they could work on the brain to relieve the pressure the blood clots were causing. That was why she could see part of your exposed brain.

The nurse finished by saying, "The doctors aren't sure yet, but they may have to put Simon into a medically induced coma for up to a week to aid and speed the healing.

As soon as she heard about the coma, a wave of desperation and fear came over her, and Vasia immediately burst into an uncontrollable fit of tears.

"Now, don't worry Mrs. Emerson, as I said before, we are fully expecting your husband to make a full recovery. He is young, fit, and healthy. He is already responding well."

"I know," Vasia said sobbing, "It's just so many wires. I've never seen him like this."

"It is a scary sight," the nurse agreed, "But he is in expert hands."

45

"How long is he going to be in there?" Vasia asked.

"If everything goes smoothly, which I reckon it will, he's got another two to three hours. Come on, I'll take you to the waiting room, and you can wait for him there. I will let you know when he's finished and in a room."

Three hours! Vasia didn't know what she was going to do for three hours that would keep her from going insane.

"Thank you," she said through grateful tears, then suddenly, a thought occurred to her, and she added, "How did this happen to him?"

The nurse looked at Vasia confused.

"You haven't heard about the terrorist attack?" she asked.

"No. What terrorist attack? I dropped everything and ran when I heard Simon was here. I wondered why the roads were busier than usual." This last comment was mostly to herself.

As the nurse led Vasia to a waiting room, she explained about the terrorist attack at Green Park just under two hours ago now. "Simon got out of one carriage relatively unscathed apart from minor cuts, but the sketchy reports that we have so far suggest that many people owe their lives to him as he stayed behind to rescue people. Vasia, he's a legitimate hero."

"You mean he was stupid and tried to play the hero?" Vasia commented angrily.

A tear came to her eye, meaning that she wasn't really that angry with you, just upset and emotional, as most wives would about their spouses. Secretly she felt a sliver of pride when she heard you tried to save people.

The waiting room contained nothing more than a dozen blue plastic chairs, a single potted plant, and a wide-screen television on the far wall. Although there wasn't anyone else in the room, the last person had left the TV on tuned to the BBC News Channel.

The current subject was the terrorist attack at Green Park Underground station. On the screen was a bird's-eye view of the streets above, looking down at the big crater opening into the disaster zone.

The nurse left Vasia alone to watch the TV before disappearing back to the operating theatre.

Although she could see that it was on and was vaguely aware of the subject, Vasia hardly watched it as she delved deeply into her own thoughts.

At one point she leant forward and held her head in her hands as a tear ran down her cheek. She clasped her hands against her mouth as if she wanted to prevent herself from throwing up and made some strangled noises. Eventually, she couldn't hold in any longer. The dams broke and she started sobbing uncontrollably. In that moment, she felt so utterly alone and helpless. Although the nurse had tried her best to soothe her worries, she couldn't help but still expect the worst.

Chapter 7

At some point, all the crying must have exhausted Vasia enough to send her asleep because the next thing she remembered was a gentle tap on the shoulder rudely pulling her out of a nice deep sleep.

Awake, it took her a few moments to get her bearings before she remembered where she was. Panic accelerated the push of adrenaline through my body.

"Is he ok?" She immediately asked the nurse standing patiently to the side of her.

"He is out of the operating theatre, and is now in his own room in ICU," the nurse reported.

After Vasia jumped up with what must seem like overly optimistic happiness, the nurse added, "We have had to put him into a medically induced coma to help him recover from the swelling."

"But he will be alright, won't he?" It was more of a plea than a question.

"Yes, he will be in a coma for at least a week, but he is well and on the mend."

"Can I see him?"

"Of course." The nurse smiled gently.

The nurse gently guided Vasia out of the room and to your private room. They took the lift two floors and had to walk what seemed miles before they eventually got there.

All the while they were walking, the nurse was chatting away to Vasia but she was only half-listening to the conversation.

Towards the end of the walk, in a reassuring tone, the nurse told her not to be shocked by the state that you were in as you had a bandage wrapped around your head. Or not to fear all the wires coming out of you and the noise of the machines.

"They're all doing their job," the nurse explained, "They're all helping him heal and keep him alive."

They got to your room, and with her hand on the door handle, the nurse turned to Vasia saying, "Spend as long as you want in there, I will be back in an hour to check his vitals."

"Thank you," Vasia said gratefully.

The nurse opened the door, and Vasia walked in. After the nurse closed the door, she found herself in a fluorescent-lit, whitewashed, windowless room.

There was a small flat-screen TV on the wall switched off, two blue high-backed chairs, a lonely potted Ficus tree in the left-hand corner, and on the right, there was a door that presumably led to the bathroom.

Vasia didn't notice any of these things at first. Probably in a state of shock, despite the nurse's warning she stood firmly in one spot staring at you looking helpless with a bandage around your head asleep in a regulation hospital bed. They had linked you to a machine console via various drips and wires. There was a screen showing your heartbeat and other numbers that meant nothing to the untrained eye. The machine was making slow, measured beeping noises and the occasional hiss.

Vasia walked over to the left side of the bed. Reaching for your hand, she gently squeezed it secretly, hoping that you would squeeze it back.

"Hello, Simon," She croaked.

Her voice sounded strange to her, almost alien, and, even though she tried her best to smile, she felt a couple of tears roll down her face.

"Look at the trouble you've got yourself into." She tried to make a feeble attempt at humour and forced out a fake laugh, but it came out as more of a snort.

Always one for small talk. Hey, what woman isn't! She tried conversing with you. However, considering it was one-sided, the choice of topics quickly disappeared. It may have been the setting because she has never enjoyed being in hospitals.

Eventually, she resorted to sitting down in one chair and continued to hold your hand and eagerly looked at your face to watch out for any sign of you waking up.

Missing your cheeky smile and goofy laugh her mind inevitably wandered towards thinking about the glorious moments in your lives. Most noticeably the first time you met.

*

"I think I remember." I suddenly interrupt

"You do?" The bearded man asks.

All though it was a question there was a knowing smile on his lips that made me feel a little weirded out.

"Yes." I say confidently.

"Tell me."

"Ok here goes…"

"Originally from Iran, Vasia had come to the UK with her family when she was just a few weeks old.

She and I had met at college, and it had been love at first sight. Well, for me, it was anyway.

I won't lie; our relationship had been filled with turmoil right from the start and still can be. Such as it was with any interracial relationship. However, outside sources created most of this turmoil.

Apart from me being an atheist...

"Nobody's perfect!" The man murmers to himself

...which would typically create enormous differences anyway, the relationship seemed to work, as we accepted, embraced, and even encouraged each other in each one's beliefs.

Vasia is taller than the norm. She is an inch or two taller than me by a few inches and curvy. Both aspects she is conscious of and can make her a little sensitive. I always try to make her smile by regularly saying she's beautiful.

We met when we were both at Sixth Form College. For months I admired her from afar and Vasia, the same with me. We would be in our own groups of friends talking and laughing with each other and Vasia would catch me staring over at her. Every time she noticed this she would often give me a sly sideways glance, nervously smile and twirl a locket of hair with a finger as she did so. Being a teenager and a Muslim teenager at that she thought this action was the height of seduction. I admit I did actually feel my heart miss a beat every time I saw her do that. Although she suspects it was more than my heart missing a beat! And she's right!

My stares were blatantly obvious. So much so that my best friend Zack who I think I might still be friends with now despite him not being Vasia's favourite person. He noticed and after looking in the direction that I was, whispered to me. "I wouldn't go there mate, she is not worth the trouble"

Zack was controversially referring to Vasia's heritage and the problems that we would face if we saw each other. Hence the reason he's not Vasia's favourite person.

However, I was only thinking one thing. Well, two if you count the fact that I thought Zack was a bit of a plonker for saying such a thing and I made sure he knew it.

No, I was thinking I had to see her no matter what.

It was actually several months of staring at each other from afar before we both picked up the courage to speak to one other.

One day I was running late for one of my classes and was hurrying down a corridor to reach the classroom when I rounded the corner and bumped into Vasia coming the other way. We had collided with such force that she fell backward and landed on her coccyx. She had been carrying some textbooks which went flying everywhere.

"Oh my God," I said horrified and immediately rushed to Vasia and knelt down to see if she was all right. "I'm so sorry."

Propping herself up on her elbows for a moment I got lost staring in her dark dreamy eyes. Vasia must have felt the same because there was a pause too long to be polite as she stared up at me. Then seemingly remembering herself and sounding sassy, she replied: "You should be, you big oaf."

Even though she had uttered an insult, she smiled a little. That same smile she would use when we are staring at each other from afar. To be so honest, on my part, I was so infatuated with her I took the insult as a term of endearment.

After what seemed like several uncomfortable, awkward seconds with her still on the floor and the two of us staring into each other's eyes, Vasia suddenly asked. "Well, are you going to help me up then?"

All at once I remembered my manners, and I put my hand out to help her up. I still remember how soft and warm her hand felt in mine. But it had a firmness that implied her strength. Once she was up and dusting herself down, I picked up the fallen textbooks and handed them back to her.

"I am sorry for knocking you down," I repeated, tensely apologetic.

"I should hope so?" Vasia said, trying to keep up her pretence of sass. "But you can make it up to me."

"Of course," I replied eager to please. Then slightly confused. "Umm… how?"

Ripping a piece of paper from one of her textbooks, she started writing something.

"You can take me out for dinner sometime," Vasia answered with way more assertiveness than she had intended.

"Umm… ok." Was my response, her forthrightness confusing me.

She handed me the piece of paper. "This is my number. Call me when you think you can stop knocking people over," she said as she started walking down the corridor. "Or when you think you're done staring at me." She added over her shoulder.

And then she disappeared. I stood there for a while looking confused but finally it dawned on me that I had just scored a date with the most beautiful girl in the college. Doing a little jig I turned round and with more of a bounce in my step I walked towards the class that I was still late for.

And as the saying goes the rest is history. We are still together more than a decade later. Vasia believes she is still the same assertive and sassy self which keeps me on my toes. Being the literal Goddess of Beauty I think her assertiveness and sass are just some of the qualities I love about her. Sometimes I would start an argument just to appreciate the comebacks she fires back my way."

"Good." The bearded man suddenly says. "You're beginning to remember."

"Yes, some. I remember my life with Vasia right up to the day of the train accident. But despite what you have been telling me I don't actually remember the day itself. I still have no idea how I got from being in a coma in hospital to here. I have no idea how I keep healing from fatal wounds. And I have no idea who you are or how you intimately know my story."

"All will become clear in due course." The man assures me.

*

Vasia lost track of the time, sitting there alone with her musings. The nurse coming in to check on your vitals rudely pulled her out of them

While she busied herself in doing her checks, Vasia slipped out of the room for a few minutes.

She went to the bathroom to powder her nose and afterward, she called both her parents and your father, Ron to let them know what was going on.

You probably know this already; Your mum had passed away two years back and, as your dad was now living in Edinburgh since her passing, he vowed that he would catch the night train into London and would be there in the morning.

Vasia's parents who also live in Luton, a couple of miles away from you, said that they were dropping everything and coming to the hospital right away. They would be there within the hour despite her saying that she was ok handling everything.

Vasia took a deep, refreshing breath. The stale sterile hospital air somehow felt good. After making the calls she re-entered your room. Instead of the nurse, there were two black Africans in tribal gear. One was a young, attractive female, and the other was an elderly male. They were both standing over you, staring solemnly down. Both were dressed in colourful clothing, a painful contrast to the dimly lit whitewashed room, and their moods, sombre. Vasia stopped in her tracks struck by the surreality of the scene in front of her. She suspected they sneaked in because only next of kin were allowed at this point.

The female was the first to look up and noticed Vasia standing there.

She smiled radiantly and walked around the bed so she could face Vasia directly.

She said, "Hello, my name is Ermee and this is my grandfather, Eraaf. You must be Simon's wife?"

She offered her hand to Vasia.

"I am," Vasia answered, shaking Ermee's hand wearily. "I'm Vasia,"

She was wondering who these two people were and how the hell you knew them. She was suspicious, and it must have shown on her face because without being prompted, Ermee said, "We were on the same train, and I got knocked out when it all happened. Your husband here helped my grandfather carry me to safety. He helped many people. Your husband is a hero, Vasia."

Her genuine smile and tender, appreciative voice verified what the nurse had said hours prior. Despite being proud of you, enough to shed a tear, Vasia echoed what she said earlier to the nurse, "No, my husband is stupid, look at where all these heroics have got him."

Ermee laid a comforting hand on her shoulder, "I know it's scary now but he will be ok. The doctors have said he should be awake in a week."

"I know, it just scares me I almost lost him, and he put himself in that situation."

"He committed a selfless act, Vasia. He has a kind soul."

Ermee and Vasia spoke for a further ten minutes while Eraaf stood behind Ermee looking down at you the whole time. He seemed deep in thought.

After their discussion, Ermee and Eraaf left Vasia on her own with you until sometime later when her parents came in.

They sat with her for several hours, when Vasia's father, a big hulking, intimidating man with a long bushy black beard, and a devout Muslim, performed a prayer for the sick, called a Du'a, over your body. This was despite you not being a Muslim and an Atheist.

"He may not believe in God, but He won't hold that against him." Vasia's father explained.

After two hours of gentle encouragement, Vasia's parents persuaded her to come up to the hospital canteen for a meal. After being stuck in the windowless hospital room for hours, walking down the corridor to the canteen, Vasia finally noticed the sun had drastically moved from east to west indicating it was late evening. She hadn't eaten since that morning.

After the meal Vasia and her parents continued to sit with you for a while more until Joanne , the same nurse from before, came in to say goodbye. "My shift is over but I'll be back in the morning. Get some rest at home, love." She added compassionately. "That's the best thing you can do for him right now."

You were in safe hands and there was nothing that she could do. Joanne promised her that the other doctors and nurses would call her immediately if anything changed.

With some gentle persuasion from her parents, Vasia reluctantly agreed.

As she walked to her car, it was twilight, and by the time she had driven home with her parents who had offered to stay the night with her, it was fully dark.

*

Just after midnight Eraaf hobbled down the twisting disinfectant smelling corridors of St Thomas Hospital. The bottom of his staff tapping on the floor made the only sound.

It was the graveyard shift and there were few medical staff around. Those that were, he easily hid from in a darkened room or two as they walked past.

Eventually he reached your room and he stealthily slipped in quietly shutting the door behind him.

For a moment he stood staring down at your comatose body and then with his staff glowing he held it above your head.

If anybody was outside, they would have seen an orange light growing brighter and seeping out of the cracks of the door frame. Then there was nothing.

Moments later the machines that were keeping you alive started beeping uncontrollably.

Eraaf quickly and quietly slipped out. He rounded the corner just in time before he overheard a nurse running into your room shouting "CODE BLUE! Get the doctor."

Chapter 8

An hour after first light, hot and flustered, Vasia came running into the hospital. A phone call had woken her with one nurse telling her to get to the hospital quickly as something had happened to you. The nurse hadn't elaborated on what happened. Vasia really didn't give her time to explain anyway. She immediately jumped out of bed, got dressed, threw some water over her face, jumped in the car, and sped to the hospital.

She made a beeline straight for your room.

She opened the door. Her heart sank into her stomach and she thought she was going to vomit onto the floor. You were not in your bed.

She headed for the nurses' station, but she froze mid-step when she heard the flush in the adjoining bathroom. She stood, eyes wide, staring at the bathroom door, her heart slamming against her ribs, while the audible sound of the occupant washing their hands came through the wall.

The occupant turned off the tap and presumably dried their hands. Vasia wanted to rip the door off its hinges. The anticipation was killing her. It was all she could do to call out.

She didn't know why she was holding her breath as the door to the bathroom opened.

And out you walked still dressed in a hospital gown and a bandage around your head, but other than that, you appeared fit, healthy and in high spirits. Vasia's eyes welled up.

You took three steps into the room before you noticed she was standing in the doorway. When you did, you immediately stopped and flashed one of your grins, the kind that you think was sexy in any other situation.

"Good Morning, Beautiful."

Straight to the point Vasia immediately demanded, "What are you doing?!"

"I was having a wee," was your instant reply.

Vasia looked like she had seen a ghost. "No." she said, shaking her head in disbelief. "You were in a coma last night and the nurses called me to say something happened."

Vasia seemed to be close to tears which always made you overprotective. So you stepped over to her and put a comforting hand on her shoulder.

"Yeah, I woke up," you said, smiling, overly cheery.

"Great, but how?"

Joanne the nurse came walking into the room.

"Good Morning, Vasia. I see you have already noticed the miracle."

"Yeah, I thought you said he would be in a coma for the next week."

"We all thought that," Joanne agreed. "Just after midnight last night he looked like he was going into cardiac arrest and then before the night staff could resuscitate him, he stopped and sat up wide awake."

"Is that normal?"

"It's not unheard off," Joanne said diplomatically. "But the doctors will run some tests to make sure he's ok."

"I feel fine. Terrific even," You boasted.

Although afraid to admit you were slightly freaked out about the coma thing and a little miffed about being talked about in 3rd person.

"That's the point. You shouldn't be," the nurse answered.

You opened your mouth to retort but a knock at the door made the three of you turn to a man in his early sixties. He was the spitting image of you, but with silver-grey hair and a more weathered face.

"Dad!" You exclaimed, genuinely surprised. "What

are you doing here?"

Your dad, Ron, smiled and stepped into the room to hug you before he answered.

"Vasia called me," he explained. "She said you were in that terrorist incident on the underground and you were in a coma. But you seem to be perfectly fine to me," he added.

"Yes, he was in a coma, but he woke up last night," Vasia explained, somewhat confused.

"The doctors think it's nothing short of a miracle," Joanne added repeating herself. "But we have a few tests lined up today to see what's going on."

*

In fact, it was more than a few. The morning was filled with test after test. At one point your room looked like a revolving door. Then the rest of the day and into the evening was spent waiting for the results.

The first was an x-ray of your head, where the injuries were already showing signs of healing. Then there was an MRI scan followed by a CT scan to check for tumours. Once they ran out of brain scans and found nothing abnormal, they threw in an Ultrasound and an Echocardiogram too, but your heart and other organs were fine. This left the doctors with a great deal of head scratching.

By the time the doctors had given up on their tests, the night was drawing in. You felt depressingly bored with all the prodding, poking and waiting around.

You seemed healthy. Which, according to the doctors, was the issue. They advised you should stay overnight so they could monitor you.

"Can I stay with Simon?" Vasia asked

"I suppose there is no harm." One of the doctors agreed somewhat reluctantly. "But don't over tire him."

61

"I will book myself into a cheap B&B for the night." Ron had said.

After he left, Vasia and you laid cuddling on the hospital bed, chatting with the TV on in the background. It was on the BBC news channel and the subject was still the terrorist attack on Green Park tube station.

Picking up from our phone conversation after the job interview, Vasia suddenly asked: "Did you really tell that interviewer he was a joke?"

"Yeah?" you answered.

You started feeling defensive. On the phone call Vasia had bent your ear over that, so what would happen now. You needn't have worried though as she started laughing. "I wish I had seen his face."

Relaxing and chuckling yourself you said, "It was a picture, I can tell you."

On TV there was some analysis, complete with CCTV pictures and artist impressions, going on about the timeline from when the terrorist boarded the train to when he got off and then the resulting explosion. They even showed CCTV imaging from inside the train, showing from the moment the man in the green hoodie left the backpack on the seat and there was a clear picture of you. Shouting after the man and going to the bag to see what was in it, you were being hailed as an ordinary bystander performing extraordinary heroic acts.

It showed the resulting chaos as people went running up and down the carriages to run away from the bomb and then the camera went dark as the bomb exploded.

Immediately solemn and looking concerned Vasia asked "How did it feel being in that?"

Watching it all back was slightly surreal for you. Your memory of it all was foggy and what you could remember was in staggering bite-sized chunks.

"They seem like small, rapid flashes." You said as

you tried to explain to Vasia "The first flash is the green-hooded figure getting off the train. The second flash is the character pulling a phone out of his pocket as the train pulled away from the station. The third flash is looking into the bag which I can't remember walking up to. And the fourth flash is more of a feeling of fear and adrenaline building up inside me and then shouting at the rest of the people on the train to run. I can't even remember what I was thinking at that point. It was as if I was on autopilot or something took over my body. I only vaguely remember waking up upside down and then getting out of the train to help some people."

As you said all this Vasia was nodding empathetically.

"Remember when I told you I had been in a car accident when I was a kid?" she said "I learnt that tragic accidents like this can play havoc with memory recall. It's all normal"

*

After a while Vasia fell asleep, leaving you wide awake, contemplating, and channel surfing.

At one point a male nurse came in to check on your vitals and before he left again, he advised you to get some sleep.

Sleep, however, seemed to escape from you tonight or so it seemed. At some point, you think you must have fallen asleep because of the dream.

In the dream, you exited your hospital room and walked down the corridor. The male nurse, the same one that told you to go to sleep, walked past, and nodded distractedly. You returned the nod and carried on walking.

You went past the nurse's station where a male and female nurse quietly huddled over a card game. They didn't bother to look up when you walked past.

63

You came to the major part of the ward. It was a big open area with a dozen hospital beds all filled with sleeping patients apart from one, a bespectacled elderly man reading a book under a night light. Engrossed in his book, you noticed it was the latest *Stephen King*.

You crossed the ward to where the corridor started again. Along here there were more private rooms. You were about to pass the first one when the door opened seemingly on its own.

You stopped and stared into the room. It was pitch black, but you could make out the rough outline of a person in the shadows walking towards you.

Because it's what you do in dreams, for some inexplicable reason you started sweating and felt a shot of panic go through you, but you couldn't move from the spot as the shape came nearer.

The shape stopped just in the doorway where there was just enough light penetrating the darkness to reveal the face of the person.

You instantly recognised the face as belonging to Eraaf but you didn't feel very much relieved. Eraaf uttered one cryptic sentence."When you're ready to have your questions answered, come find me."

Then he stepped back into the shadows and vanished with the door closing, seemingly on its own volition.

You stood like the Queen's guard for a few moments, transfixed on the closed door.

Then shrugging your shoulders, you carried on up the hallway.

You reached the last private room, and, noticing a light coming from it, you peered through the small square window in the door.

The room inside was much like your own, apart from this one had windows overlooking the London streets outside.

There was a middle-aged man with curly black hair asleep in his bed with machines beeping around him.

You're not sure why you did it, but you opened the door to the private room and, only giving the man in the bed a cursory glance, you crossed the room to the window and peered out.

It was nighttime, and apart from the Thames and the iconic Palace of Westminster across the river, there wasn't much to see. You saw a few cars driving over Westminster Bridge.

After a while, you had the distinct feeling that someone was watching you and you turned your head in the direction of the man's bed.

Except the man wasn't in his bed anymore.

He was standing right beside, facing you.

Startled, you jumped back and your back hit the wall.

As he was standing, you thought surely he must be awake, but you quickly noticed his eyes were closed.

A second later, waterfalls of blood started flowing out of both sides of the man's mouth.

You were both horrified, disgusted and mesmerised as the man's mouth opened. He looked like he was trying to scream but he couldn't. His mouth was full of blood.

His eyes opened the colour of egg whites.

He reached out for you. You panicked, wanting to get as far away as you could but you couldn't move

A sudden piercing noise interrupted the moment.

You looked over to the machines and saw it was them making the noise. The man was flatlining.

You looked back at the man, who was trying to say something. Through all the blood it sounded like "Help me"

At that point, you sat bolt upright in your bed. Vasia stirred a bit but did not wake up.

For long moments you just sat staring at the wall

trying to get your breathing under control. Your heart was hammering like an express train and you were sweating profusely.

After a while, you swung your legs round to the edge of the bed and put your feet on the cold tiled floor.

With a heavy sigh, you put your head in your hands.

"Shit, that was some strange dream." You quietly cursed to yourself.

You looked up through the open doorway into the hallway in time to see the male nurse who had told you to go to sleep, walk past. He saw you and gave a quick nod before he walked out of eyesight.

Feeling a powerful sense of Deja vu, you stood up and walked out of your room and into the corridor.

You looked in the direction the nurse went in, but he had already disappeared around the corner.

You looked the other way and after a moment of deliberation you made your way up the corridor.

You passed the nurses' station where there was a male and female nurse playing a card game. A nasty feeling bottomed out deep down in the pit of your stomach.

You continued up the corridor until it opened into the main ward. There were a dozen beds all filled with sleeping patients apart from one.

You felt a moment of disorientation remembering your dream. You expected the person to be a bespectacled elderly man. Instead, it was a bespectacled elderly woman reading a *Catherine Cookson* novel.

She must have sensed you staring at her because she looked up, gave you a distracted smile, and returned to her book.

You didn't smile back. You were busy trying not to freak out.

A moment of inspiration made you go to the room that Eraaf had come out of.

You yanked the door open and... A cleaning

cupboard. There was nothing in there apart from buckets, mops, brooms, and other cleaning paraphernalia.

On the far wall there was a fading, peeling poster with the famous "Keep Calm" slogan on. Finding the "Cause Shit Happens" message below it ironic, you shut the door, half disgusted.

It was then that you saw the door to the last private room. You stood there for a moment not knowing what to do.

Eventually, you decided. Walking up to it, you peered through the window.

For several moments you just stood staring into the room, not able to breathe. The scene was exactly the same as what you had seen in your dream. A room much like yours but with windows looking out on the Thames and the Palace of Westminster.

There was also a middle-aged curly-haired man asleep in bed.

After a while when nothing seemed to happen, you felt like you could be able to breathe again, and you chuckled at yourself for being silly.

You were about to look away and walk back to your room when the man suddenly started convulsing. On the foot of that, the machines began letting out a piercing alarm.

You stared open-mouthed as the nurses came sprinting up and rushed into the room, rudely shoving you aside. A third nurse, the one that had told you to get some sleep, also went in but not before ordering you to go back to your room. He closed the door to the room and closed the blinds so nobody could see in. You just had time to see that the first two nurses had taken the sides down on the bed and were trying to resuscitate the man.

You stared at the blinded window for a second. Then trying to grasp what had just happened, lost in thought, you trudged back up to your room.

On your way back you watched a female doctor rush past you and into the man's room. She didn't bother closing the door behind her as the nurse had.

As you entered your room, you heard the doctor giving a time of death.

Chapter 9

Several hours later and it was daylight.

After last night's events, sleep was not a luxury.

Despite that, you were feeling jovial and had changed out of your regulation hospital gown into a pair of black jeans and navy-blue t-shirt that your dad had brought you after he had left the hospital the night before.

The playful demeanour could have been down to the fact that the doctors had just given you a clean bill of health and said you could go home. Although, they wanted you to book an appointment to see your GP within the next week for a checkup.

While you were waiting for Vasia to freshen up in the bathroom and your dad had popped to the visitors' bathroom down the hallway, Joanne came in to say goodbye and wish you luck for the future.

Having not told Vasia or your dad about what happened last night, you took the opportunity to quietly ask the nurse about the man in the far private room.

"Unfortunately, he had a cardiac arrest and died," Joanne said sadly, and then, looking confused, she asked, "How did you know about him?"

"Oh, I heard the alarm on his machine from here and saw the doctors and nurses run into his room. There was quite a commotion," you answered trying to stick to the truth as much as possible.

The answer seemed to satisfy Joanne. With the arrivals of Vasia and your dad, the discussion changed.

The four of you said your last goodbyes. Vasia even gave Joanne a tearful yet appreciative hug. We were then free to leave.

Just as we got to the front doors, Vasia and your dad turned and looked solemnly at you. "Don't be scared," Vasia almost whispered.

That wasn't cryptic or confusing at all.

"Don't be scared of what?" you asked with a sinking feeling in my stomach, but Vasia had already turned and was exiting through the doors.

You followed with some trepidation, into the bright sunlit outdoors, with your dad following quickly behind.

It took your eyes a while to adjust after being in the fluorescent-lit hospital for two days. Your first thought was you were seeing an unusually sizable group of people standing by the entrance.

As your eyes grew more accustomed to the daylight, you noticed most of these people had a variety of videography and camera equipment and some had microphones - the paparazzi. You even knew a few peoples' faces from the TV.

The paparazzi as one organism, it seemed, turned to you. You felt a pang of growing fear, deep in your stomach, that could be likened to the phrase 'rabbit caught in headlights.'

You couldn't tell what happened in what order, but cameras started flashing, video cameras started rolling and journalists fired questions as they rammed microphones up your nose.

"Mr. Emerson," one shouted. "Fergal Keane. BBC News. How does it feel being the hero of the hour?"

"Mr. Emerson," another hollered. "Tessa Chapman. 5 News. How did it feel being in the train crash?"

"Mr. Emerson. Rhiannon Mills. Sky News. How did it feel facing the terrorist?"

Various reporters screamed more questions at you leaving you at a loss for words and completely overwhelmed.

So, it was left to both Vasia and Dad to grab your arms and practically drag you through the scrum of reporters and to the red Vauxhall Astra that you and Vasia share.

Vasia hurriedly unlocked the car, and the three of you climbed in with you riding shotgun. You were about to duck your head into the car when you heard another reporter repeat the same question about how it felt to be a hero.

You paused.

You remembered thinking at the time that that was the most mindless question ever. Feeling embarrassed, awkward and annoyed for some reason too, you turned to the reporter. "I'm not a hero." You said quietly
And with that, you quickly got in the car and Vasia drove as fast as she could through the crowd of reporters and flashing cameras. She raced through the congested, noisy London streets and up the M1 to your home in Luton.

You were expecting to see paparazzi outside your home too, but thankfully there weren't any, and the three of you got into the relative safety of your house without incident.

Chapter 10

Although it was understood that you should rest, a few hours after being home, you were more fidgety than a college student who sloshed back a pot of black coffee and two energy drinks..

"If it's all the same, I'm going to get the night train back to Edinburgh tonight." Your dad said.

So you suggested, "Okay dad, how about we grab a pint before then?"

Dad and Vasia both showed some concern regarding your health, but after some gentle persuasion, the three of you inevitably found yourselves in *The Kings Arms*.

Zack, your best friend from college, was there as he usually was these days. It showed with his beer gut and permanent greasy appearance—a product of alcohol sweats.

The four of you were all drinking and playing pool with Dad and Zack teaming up against Vasia and yourself. It was soon undeniable that Vasia and you were the dream team and had won so many games you had lost count.

Twice when you went to the bar to get your round in, you discovered that you didn't need to pay as other patrons at the pub who recognised you from the news, were offering to pay, calling you a hero and clapping you on the back for a job well done.

"Do you know who you are?" One sweaty, balding stranger managed to slur amid a few hiccups and belches. With breath that could strip wallpaper, he had clearly already had too much to drink. He was overly familiar with you with his arm around you. He had a pint of lager in his other hand which he was managing to spill a little on your chest as he pointed at while he spoke.

Despite all this you were still in a pleasant mood

and deciding to humour the man you answered. "No, who am I?"

"A warrior."

"Really?

"Yeah the way you faced down that terrorist…"

"I didn't actually face him down."

"And you saved all those people." he carried on ignoring you. "You are a bonafide hero. Let me buy you a drink."

Despite your earlier issue with the reporters calling you a hero and finding the entire thing embarrassing, you quickly cottoned on that if you could get a free pint or two out of it, it wasn't all that bad.

Before long, it was dark outside, and it was time to head home. After losing the last game, Zack threw the pool cue down onto the pool table in mock disgust.
"Ok, I know when I'm beaten," he declared.

Zack then made his excuses and went to the toilet. A moment later, you followed him.

You were both standing at the urinals, side by side, but not talking, as men rarely do as an unwritten rule. You started feeling dizzy and went to grab the wall with your free hand to steady yourself. But the wall wasn't there. It took you a moment to realise that you were no longer standing at the urinal in the toilet of *The Kings Arms*. In fact, you were on the pavement outside of *The Kings Arms*.

"What the fuck?" was your first reaction after you had done your fly up.

You looked at your watch. It was still nine o'clock, so no time had passed.

After the initial shock, you started wondering how much you had been drinking.

"I guess I must have drunk too much." you said to yourself. You shrugged your shoulders and turned to go back to the pub.

The springtime weather in the UK had forced

everybody who was out in the relative warmth of where they were going. In this case the pub, nobody wanted to be in the beer garden or the smokers corner when it was cold, especially with a fine drizzle blanketing everything as it was on this night. The roads were almost as empty as the beer garden.

So when a young, attractive woman ran past you, you were surprised. Despite the cold and rain she was wearing a skimpy, sparkly blue dress indicating she was on a night out.

Visibly upset and screaming, she kept looking back over her shoulder.

"Huh?" You looked back in the direction the woman had come in time to see two men in dark hoodies running after her.

The woman hadn't noticed you despite almost knocking you over. When the two men didn't seem to see you either, even with one of them being on a direct collision course, you started wondering if you were a ghost. You didn't have time to solve the problem.

On instinct, you put your hands out to stop the man. The hoodie obscured his face, but he looked like he was white with a week's worth of stubble.

It was too late; the man went into you.

And through you.

And came out the other side and carried on running.

Maybe you were a ghost!

"What the fuck?" You screamed. The feeling of the man running through you caused a weird cold sensation to travel through your body.

Shaking the feeling off, you turned around in time to see the two men catch up with the woman and shove her to the floor.

The biggest of the two men picked her up, and, standing behind her, had one hand over her mouth to stop her screams and the other hand restraining her arms behind her. He was obviously strong, but still, she struggled. The struggling that happened from someone who knew their life was about to end.

The second man advanced on the woman, an evil grin on his face, he stood inches away from the lady's face. You didn't want to imagine what his breath smelled like. You watched as he whispered something in her ear. Something you couldn't hear, but her panicked reaction screamed volumes. Tears welled up as she tried to plead through the first man's hand.

In one swift movement, the second man ripped the front of the lady's blue sparkly dress, and with his knife, sliced through her satin bra with as much resistance as a birthday candle in a summer storm.

The man stood leering at her exquisite physique. Her hard breathing chest jiggled her breasts.

Horrified, you realised what was about to happen.

Quickly getting over the shock of being run through you sprinted towards the trio, yelling at the men to stop, "OYE, BLOKES, BUGGER OFF!!!"

The men hadn't heard or seen you coming towards them. The second man was undoing his fly when you went to rugby tackle him to the floor.

The chilly sensation happened again. You passed right through him and landed face first in the gravel.

You turned over in time to see the first man undoing his fly. He had to let go of the lady's mouth to do so. As soon as he did, she started screaming. This earned her a hefty slap across the face from the second man. The slap was so hard that the woman looked dizzy for a moment.

Now both men had their flies undone and their dicks out. The one in front roughly grabbed the lady by the chin. He leaned in as if to kiss her. The lady tried to move her face in disgust, but the man planted a massive kiss on her lips. He tried to give her tongue, but the woman bit him. The man didn't seem to mind; in fact, he looked like he appeared to enjoy it.

Laughing, both men moved in to penetrate her from both ends. The lady started screaming in terror.

You screamed too and tried to stand up.

Suddenly the trio wasn't there. Or depending on which way you look at it, you weren't where the trio was.

Dizzy, you grabbed the wall above the urinal to steady yourself. You looked around for the trio but you were back in the pub toilet.

By now, Zack was washing his hands at the sink, and noticed you looking unsteady.

"I think you might have had a few too many?" he said to you, laughing, but stopped when his friend turned around and noticed the strange look on your face.

"What's the matter?" Zack asked, suddenly concerned.

You didn't answer. Absentmindedly doing up your fly, you walked across the toilet floor to the exit and walked out to the bar.

Vasia and your dad were sitting by the pool table, talking, laughing, and sipping their drinks when they noticed you purposefully walk out of the toilet as if you were on some mission. You stopped and stood by the pool table. You looked out of the window to the street with a strange, expectant look on your face.

"What's up?" Vasia and Ron asked in unison copying Zack's sentiment

You ignored them. You stood there for a second until you saw the woman in the blue dress run past. When two men in hoodies also ran past following her, you grabbed a pool cue and ran out.

Shouts questioning your sanity from Vasia and the guys followed you,

Adrenaline pumping, you ran outside and jumped over the four foot wall separating the street from the pub's beer garden. You sprinted after the two men, arriving in time to watch them picking her up from the ground.

Without breaking your stride and brandishing the pool cue over your head, you yelled at the two men. The one in front of the lady heard you first and looked up.

In the split second before you brought your pool cue down on the man's head, you saw he was a young Hispanic man in his early twenties.

A stupid look of surprise showed on the man's face before it connected with the pool cue. The cue splintered in half, and you heard a satisfying crack as the man's nose broke, blood splattering out like grey matter all over a wall. He flew backward and hit his head on the floor. You didn't know if he was unconscious before he hit the ground or not, but you didn't really care.

You turned to the woman, still held from behind by the other attacker. She was crying but looking at you with some sense of relief. You noticed the second attacker was a young white man with dreadlocks and an unkempt goatee.

For a moment, he looked like he didn't know what to do before inspiration struck. With a heavy dose of self-preservation, he shoved the woman into you and sprinted off.

You didn't bother to chase him. You were more concerned with making sure the woman was ok.

"Yes, Yes, I am fine," the woman said.

She was backing away as if she would run. Did she think you were another attacker?

"It's ok, don't be scared. I'm not going to hurt you," you declared with your palms up to reassure the woman. You got your smartphone out of your trouser pocket and said to her, "Look, I'll call the police, and they'll help you."

That comment seemed to scare her more. "No, don't call them. I don't want any bother." she stammered.

"It won't be any bother. You need to tell the police what happened so that these men won't do it again."

"No, I don't want any bother," the woman repeated, and with that, she turned and ran.

You stared after her, feeling perplexed. Then you remembered the first attacker you had knocked out with the pool cue and was still lying unconscious on the ground.

You knelt to feel his pulse. He was still alive.

Seeing the blood gushing out of the man's nose with the shattered pool cue lying beside him, you guessed you would get into more trouble with this than the actual would-be rapist. Considering the woman who just survived the attempted rape was no longer around, it would be difficult to explain yourself. It would be a classic "he said/she said" situation when he woke up.

You instantly backed up and looked around. No witnesses were around.

Trying to look nonchalant, and whistling with your hands in your pockets, you turned around and walked back towards the pub. As inconspicuous as you thought you looked, a blindman could see you were out of place.

Back in the pub, Vasia, Zack and your dad, were getting ready to go see where you had got to and asked what had made you run out like that.

Shrugging, you quickly lied, "Thought I saw someone I knew," you said, "but I was mistaken."

Shaking their heads as if they thought you were crazy, but accepting your explanation, nevertheless, you all walked out of the pub and back to your house.

Chapter 11

Shortly after, your dad had made his way to the train station for his long journey home to Scotland. Zack had gone back home too.

By the time Vasia and you got to bed that night, the two of you were feeling emotionally shattered.

In your case, at least, you were also feeling wired from the confrontation with the would-be rapists. You weren't ready for sleep, at least not yet.

When you got into bed; you kissed Vasia on the nape of her neck. You could feel how warm her skin felt against your lips and the not overbearing smell of her perfume waffed up your nose. Your hand slid down to her left nipple and caressed it for a few moments.

Although clearly tired, Vasia did not object. Instead, she sighed deeply and let out a brief moan when you moved your hand, stroking her belly down to her womanhood and massaged her fast becoming moist clit.

After a few moments, Vasia reciprocated by sliding her hand down inside your pyjama shorts and started caressing your member.

Upon feeling her soft, delicate hands, you responded almost instantaneously. Faster than a shark attack, you were completely hard and erect.

A weird primal feeling surged from the tips of your toes to your head, and you suddenly felt light-headed as if you had vertigo.

Vasia had been looking into your eyes and noticed the change in your face.

"Honey, are you ok?" she asked momentarily concerned.

Shaking off the dizzy feeling, you eased Vasia's hand away from my manhood.

Grinning, you declared, "I don't think you need to

give me any more encouragement."

In one effortless movement, you got on top. Keeping your eyes on Vasia as she watched you, you started gently kissing, sucking, and licking her body all the way down until the feel of her pubic hair tickled your tongue and you could smell and taste her tender womanhood. She let out an involuntary moan and arched her back. You felt yourself start to throb.

Slowly at first, you licked and sucked on the folds of skin until your tongue pressed against her love button. Vasia let out another low pleasurable moan, and her back arched upwards again.

You looked up her curvy body, watching for the small telltale signs letting you know how close to orgasm she was. You pleasured her for many moments. Fluid filled your mouth. You loved it when she squirted into your mouth. It always made your erections harder. You continued on even as she was gasping and screaming in ecstasy. The screams added to your own ecstasy.

Taking the taste of her as a cue she had climaxed, you came up her body, kissing and licking her as you ascended. Knowing she couldn't bear your delay, your torture, much longer. You purposely spent some time on the erect buds of her breasts. You gave her left one a playful nip. She yelped. Her face confirmed it was more out of ecstasy than pain. You kissed her hard on the mouth and she reciprocated hungrily entwining her long hot tongue with yours.

Vasia suddenly pushed you back, and for a moment, you looked confused. Then smiling seductively, she slowly removed her black cotton nightie.

As men do, you took that as a cue, and wasting no time, you stripped yourself of your short-sleeve pyjama top and shorts and tossed them across the room paying no attention to where they landed.

For a moment you looked at each other hungrily,

like two lions about to pounce on a mouse, admiring each other's nakedness.

You went to lean into her, but she stopped you. Gently, she pushed for you to roll over.

You obliged. She spread your legs and started caressing your scrotum. She started using her finger nails to softly pull at the hairs protecting it. She opened her mouth and with her tongue, pulled your sack into her mouth. The moisture's enveloping sensation excited you to something akin to euphoria. She sucked with the same intensity that you had on her bean. When your breath increased, she released you, letting her saliva drip onto the sheets. With the speed of a slug, she licked up your throbbing shaft to your head. In one quick motion, she lapped up the fluid there. This was the part she always seemed to love. She went down on you, gently caressing your member with her tongue the occasional nip at your foreskin.

As with the handjob, you did not need her to spend long doing this. Almost immediately, you gently tugged her silky black hair to let her know she should come up.

Teasing you, she was slow about it, sucking all the way up until you fell out of her mouth. With a mischievous glint in her eye and biting the bottom of her lip, she moaned as she started rubbing your erection in between her breasts.

You started getting that weird primal feeling again and started feeling dizzy. Vasia saw it and took it as a sign that you wouldn't be able to bear it much longer.

Pulling away and gradually going up your body, rubbing your skin with her breasts and planting small kisses on your stomach, chest, and neck, she eventually reached your mouth and kissed you. Her alluring hot breath and tongue caressing yours just made you want her more.

Still feeling a little dizzy though, Vasia mounted you. The penetration was fast. You couldn't believe how

easily you slipped into her. Like a key into a lock. Vasia
was equally surprised. When you hit home, her eyes
opened wide in titillating shock. She arched her back and
lifted her head upwards, moaning in pleasure.

As soon as you felt the walls of her warm, wet
clitoris gripping your member, you too let out a breathless
moan. The vertigo feeling increased, and for a moment, you
felt like you would be sick.

Vasia started riding you slowly at first and
increased speed. You were both panting and breathing hard,
with sweat glistening on your naked bodies.

The vertigo feeling was still there, but there was
also that familiar feeling that you would cum. You tried to
concentrate on lasting for a little longer, and the vertigo
began to dissipate.

Vasia started heavy barking that turned into
screaming, but then you stopped, and in one expert
movement, you pushed Vasia up and to the side and
climbed on top of her missionary style.

You did it with a strength you didn't normally have
and, in hindsight, should have worried about.

With an animalistic urge, you penetrated Vasia
rather too roughly and earnt a gasp of surprise from her.

The gasp shook you out of my pleasure fog for a
moment.

"Sorry, are you ok?"

"Of course." Vasia answered breathlessly, "Don't
stop now." She added impatiently.

You didn't need to be told twice.

You started moving in and out with wild ferocity,
grunting with the effort. You were aware and further
encouraged by Vasia's moaning. You pounded harder into
her with every sound, every note, of her voice. Watching
her breasts jogging back and forth with the movements
slamming her always stimulated you onward.

Just as you felt yourself on the cusp of cuming, the

82

vertigo feeling came back with a vengeance.

Vasia screamed in ecstasy. She was cuming.

Ferociously, you exploded into her. You could feel your own cum splashing into her and you screamed too.

But your screams were mostly because you felt like you were on a roller coaster going straight down.

Moments later, you rolled off Vasia and to the side. For a long time, you stared at the ceiling recovering from both the lovemaking session and the vertigo feeling.

Finally, Vasia laughed and through quick breaths, "That was great. We haven't been that intense for a very long while."

"It was," you agreed, and it was no lie. Vasia moved on to her side, intertwining her legs with yours, and cuddled up to you. You could feel your own leftover ejaculate, almost hot on your leg, trickling down. Whispering in my ear, she declared, "I love you."

Kissing her on the lips and pulling her body in closer, you replied likewise.

Feeling her hot, sweaty body against yours and feeling her silky breath on your ear immediately caused you to feel aroused again.

Vasia, feeling you grow against her leg, looked up at you, shocked. "You have got to be kidding me!"

Saying nothing, momentarily forgetting the vertigo, you cheekily smiled and conspiratorially waved your eyebrows at her.

Knowing what the message meant, Vasia paused for a few moments. Then shrugging her shoulders, she gave you the come-on gesture.

You leaned in to kiss Vasia's neck, and your hand slowly made its way to her womanhood again.

*

"I know I said I wasn't going to interrupt again but I'm just going to come out and say it. It's weird that you know all that." I say to the bearded man.

"We have actually known each other for a while and you told me that story yourself once." The man responds.

"What? I told you about having sex with my wife and what we do?" I am a little skeptical.

"Umm, yes." The man stutters. "You probably don't believe it now but we share a special bond."

"What kind of special bond?" I ask wearily my mind is racing, thinking all things.

"Get your mind out of the gutter, it's not that kind of bond." The man says defensively. "If you let me tell your story it will become clear."

"Ok." I reluctantly agree.

*

Soon after you had made love for the second time. Then a third time too!

Over an hour later, the two of you were a hot sweaty mess. Despite your bodies being entangled with each other, exhausted, Vasia had fallen asleep and was gently snoring.

Usually, it is guaranteed that you would be asleep straight after making love, as is typical of a man. But you were still wide awake.

You were staring up at the ceiling with a satisfied smile on your face. You thought that was the best that you had performed together for a long while since you had first met nearly 15 years ago.

When you two first started dating at college, as was typical of youthful love, you had a very passionate affair. You were always making love for hours on end and not just indoors either. There were plenty of spots outdoors as well. Like the time you did it in your old Volkswagen Golf, in a dank multi-story car park, late at night, after seeing an xrated film at the cinema.

Or the time you went to Devon for a week and found a secluded spot on Dartmoor. You had actually had a massive argument at that time. About what? You have probably forgotten now. Something silly and unimportant now. But you made up only as a youthful, venereal couple knew how too.

After the occasion, laying in the middle of nowhere, with just the wild ponies watching on, Vasia pointed out it felt very Catherine and Heathcliff of you two.

As far as you know, no one caught you doing this despite the risk. Which just added to the excitement.

Now, married and trying for a child, the lovemaking was still great. You are both sexually active people, and you always enjoy it. But you feel it lacks the same animal intensity and raw excitement that you had experienced when you first met. Yourself, up until this moment in time, felt now that you were in your thirties, lack the stamina that you had when you were in your late teens and early twenties.

That was until this night. Doing it three times in one night was practically unheard of these days. Usually, three times in one month would have been acceptable.

Your satisfied smile eventually started turning into a slightly perplexed look. Despite the long day and the marathon session of lovemaking, You did not feel tired in the least. Sleep seemed to escape you. You closed your eyes several times but opened them minutes later, getting increasingly frustrated.

Eventually, at 3 am, you gave up trying to sleep and got up out of bed to go downstairs.

Before you did that, you popped into the bathroom to relieve yourself.

It was when you were washing your hands and looking at yourself in the mirror directly in front that you noticed something odd.

You turned your head this way and that to get a better view, but your hair looked the same.

Eventually, you leaned in to get a better look until your nose was almost touching the mirror. It was as you had first thought. Your grey hairs had all gone!

After a moment, you shrugged your shoulders, chalking it down to the lighting and went downstairs.

Chapter 12

Some hours later, it was daylight.

After Vasia had performed her morning Fajr, the two of you were at the kitchen table, eating toast and drinking a cup of tea.

You were in a bit of a weird, sombre mood that morning. Considering you had no sleep at all, which now made it two nights in a row, and you didn't feel sleepy you were beginning to get worried.

Vasia had noticed that you were quieter than usual. Chalking it down to the marathon love-making session you had last night, she rubbed your foot with hers under the table. When you looked up from your toast, she bit her lip seductively and winked at you.

Despite your worries, you couldn't help but smile. And even though it had only been a wink from her, or maybe it was her foot caressing yours, you felt that familiar tingling sensation deep in your groin.

The flat-screen TV on the wall above the dining table was on and was tuned to the Sky News Channel. You were only half paying it attention when the female news anchor started talking about the terrorist attack on the London Underground again.

She mentioned that the police had no leads, and no known terrorist organisations had claimed responsibility. Not even the usual suspects like Islamists linked to Al Qaeda or ISIS. Or any Irish republican organisations such as the IRA, or any ultra-white movements like the EDL, the English Defence League. It sounded like it stumped the police.

There were rumours that the EDL and other right-wing groups were planning demonstrations in major UK cities and towns such as London and Luton within the next four weeks. The demonstrations would be about blaming the Muslims and other minority groups for the terrorist attack.

In response to this, some Muslim groups like the MDL, the Muslim Defence League, would set up some counter-demonstrations blaming the attacks on the EDL. The news anchor commented that the situation was very sensitive now.

"No kidding," you said to yourself, distractedly.

"I was wondering when they were going to blame the Muslims." Vasia suddenly quipped.

Being a Muslim herself you knew that this kind of thing was a sensitive topic, so you had to choose your words carefully.

"I know it's bad at the moment but once they find out who actually did it, it will all be ok. Besides I don't think it was any terrorist organisation that we know of." You said.

"How's that?" Vasia asked. Her attitude was still prickly, and she had stopped massaging your foot.

"Well if it was any group linked to ISIS or Al Qaeda, they would have admitted to it already. They always do." You weakly chuckled at the point implying you were trying to lighten the mood. However, Vasia was not laughing so you quickly carried on. "Same for groups like the IRA they would have admitted to it by now as well. As for the EDL. Well it was too clinical for them."

Vasia was about to retort when the doorbell ringing interrupted her. "I'll get that." she mumbled to herself, instead.

Standing at the door were two men in tailor-made suits. One was Asian in his early twenties and looked athletic in his navy-blue suit. The other was a stocky middle-aged white man wearing a pastille grey number.

The older and more intimidating of the two, asked, "Mrs. Emerson?"

"Yes?" Vasia answered with a slight weariness.

Both men got what looked like leather wallets out of their pockets and flipped them open for Vasia to see the badges.

"I'm Detective Stone from Scotland Yard," the older man announced. "And my partner here is Special Agent Haider, FBI liaison officer to Scotland Yard. Is your husband home?"

"He is," Vasia answered wearily. "I guess you want to talk to him about the terrorist attack in London?"

"Yes, may we come in?" asked Detective Stone, trying to smile, but it came out as more of a grimace.

"Yeah, sure, come in." Vasia showed the detective and the FBI liaison officer in and was about to pop her head into the kitchen to tell you the police were in when you came walking out. You had overheard and seen what had been going on from the kitchen table. So on the alert, you immediately stood up and exited the kitchen.

You greeted the two men with a handshake each and the four of you filed into the living room.

"Please make yourselves feel comfortable." You said to the detectives.

While they planted themselves in one of the two black two-seater sofas, Vasia took their drink order and disappeared off to the kitchen leaving you on your own with the two lawmen exchanging awkward pleasantries.

"So. Are you two into football?" You asked.

"American or English? Haider countered.

Minutes later, Vasia walked back in with a tray of three cups of coffee and a tea for you, with a container of sugar and a small jug of milk.

You had made myself comfortable in the other two-seater sofa opposite the two men and were still attempting to make small talk with them with only a slight hint of uncomfortableness in the air.

Haider, with the slight twang of a New York accent, was in the middle of apologising for intruding on you in your home, "The doctors wouldn't let us talk to you while you were in the hospital, fearing that they would place unnecessary stress on you." he explained

Vasia sat the tray down on the oak effect Ikea coffee table in the middle of the sofas, and after telling everyone to help themselves, she plonked herself down on the couch beside you.

"No, I don't mind. Any help I can give to catch the people who did this."

"Good." Stone said as he proceeded to reach for some sugar to put in his coffee and stir it in.

"Some of our questions may seem personal and bizarre, but please don't get stressed out."

Haider took a slim black and silver dictaphone out of his suit jacket inside pocket and asked, "Do you have any objections to us recording this?"

"No, I don't mind," you answered. Secretly you were feeling slightly awkward, and with the events of last night at the pub still fresh in your mind, there was an irrational feeling of paranoia and guilt.

Stone switched the dictaphone on and spoke into it. "This is Detective Eddie Stone and Special Agent Elias Haider speaking to Mr. Simon Emerson regarding the terrorist attack on the London Underground on 16th March this year. Also present is Simon's wife, Vasia Emerson."

The detective sat the dictaphone in the middle of the coffee table, so it was directly between you. "Now Mr. Emerson." the detective continued, "how did you come to be on that particular train that day?"

"I was in London, attending a job interview. I was actually on my way back home from the interview."

"Who was the interview with?"

"It was a computer systems firm called IntelliTech. I was applying for an analyst role."

"Were you successful?"

"I don't know," you answered, thinking about how

you had walked out. "They said they should let me know in a few days."

"Ok, hope you get the job." Stone said.

Even though Stone sounded perfunctory rather than sincere, you thanked him anyway.

"Now think back to what happened on the train. Can you tell us what was going on before the explosion? Any people or things that you thought might be out of place or weird at the time? Anything really, regardless of how small or trivial, it all helps with our investigation."

You launched into your account of what happened. When you mentioned the man in the green hoodie, the detectives stopped you and asked questions about the stranger.

"What did this man look like?"

"I don't know, his hoodie covered most of his face, I couldn't see it at all."

"Was he white? Asian? Black?"

"I don't know. I can't say for sure."

"How tall was he?"

"Don't know."

"Was he my height? Taller? Shorter?"

"Maybe the same height as I am, give or take an inch or two."

"Ok, what about his clothes? Did you notice if they were branded with words or pictures?"

"No, his clothes were totally plain."

"What about smells? Did he smell of anything? BO? Antiperspirant? Cheap cologne?"

"No, I didn't notice any smells, apart from the usual Underground smells."

The two detectives spent several moments writing something in their notepads and then asked for you to carry on with your account.

And you did carry on with your account. You included getting knocked unconscious and waking up next to a dead lady that you had tried to save. You also added how you climbed out of the train, and afterwards, the explosion and getting knocked unconscious again.

You were only interrupted twice by the two detectives who asked you to clarify a few things, and forty-five minutes later, the interview was over. FBI Liaison Officer Haider switched off the dictaphone and put it back in his inside suit jacket pocket.

"Well, I think that's it," Haider said as the two men stood up. "Do you have questions for us?"

"Only one," You remarked. "No offence, but why is the FBI involved? You're far from home." You tried to add a brief laugh to the end of the last comment to imply you were joking, but it fell flat out of nervousness.

"Can't really say much because of how sensitive the situation is, but I was already on secondment to Scotland Yard, and this investigation warrants international involvement."

You absentmindedly gave a nod to show that you understood, but in reality, you didn't

"If you have any more questions or remember anything, let us know," Detective Stone was saying as they walked up the hallway to the front door.

"I will, I wish I could have been more helpful," you said apologetically as Vasia and you also stood to show the two detectives to the door.

As the four of you got to the door, Stone noticed a white rectangular envelope on the carpet that must have been posted through the letterbox while you were all talking. He stooped down to get it, and after giving the name and address a short, cursory glance, he handed it to you. Without thinking, you just put in your jeans pocket, paying it less attention than the detective did.

"You were a significant help," Stone said. "Cameras weren't so great showing the bomber, and they were in black and white, so you just telling us the man was wearing a green hoodie is a significant break for us."

"Do you have any idea who could have done this?" Vasia asked.

"We're not at liberty to discuss the investigation because of how sensitive the situation is," Stone said repeating what Haider had said earlier. "However, to be truthful, we do not know who it is yet." He continued, "Nobody has claimed responsibility for it. We don't know if it's a terrorist organisation or just some individual with a grudge against the London Underground. However, as usual, everybody's blaming the Muslims, and the Muslims are blaming everyone else."

You did a quick sideways glance at Vasia as Stone made that comment. She was doing a fantastic job hiding it with a pleasant enough smile, but with years of being together and following your conversion in the kitchen before the detectives came, you knew she had found that comment offensive. She was most likely thinking the detective was a giant douche for saying such a thing.

Vasia opened the door to let the detectives out. Haider produced a business card and handed it to you. "If you remember any more," he repeated, "call us, anytime."

"I will," you promised.

The detective and special agent walked out of the house, and the door closed behind them.

*

Stone and Haider walked over to where they had parked their black BMW I8 and climbed in with Stone in the driver's seat.

Stone put the key in the ignition but didn't turn it. Instead, he sat back, looking thoughtful.

"You're thinking the same thing I am, aren't you?" Haider queried.

"With a massive head wound, he was in critical

93

condition a few days ago, but yet there was no scratch on him that I could see," Stone answered, rubbing his chin.

"Exactly," Haider said.

"Haider, I think we will have to keep a close eye on Mr. Emerson. There's something he's hiding."

Haider answered with a conspiratorial nod.

Stone started the engine, and they drove away.

Chapter 13

After closing the door, Vasia turned to you with her eyebrows raised, "Wow, that was awkward."

"They were a bit highly strung," you agreed.

"Never mind, it's all over now," Vasia said as she stepped over to you and kissed you.

Although it was meant to be just reassuring, you immediately returned the kiss passionately. You put your hand on the small of Vasia's back and pulled her in closer as the familiar feeling of desire started bubbling away.

Vasia must have felt your bulge growing down below because she pulled away with what looked like some reluctance.

"You have got to be kidding me," she said, with a brief chuckle. "Two police officers have just questioned you and after last night too."

For a few moments, you did wonder yourself why you were so turned on all of a sudden. All you could do was grin sheepishly.

"I have to get to work, so haven't got time," Vasia continued, sounding a little despondent about it. She grabbed her coat and handbag.

"But keep that thought for tonight," she smiled and gave you another peck on the mouth. When she pulled away this time, she had a serious look on her face.

"Are you going to be ok on your own?"

"Of course," you answered, laughing. "I'm an adult."

"I know, but you were in a coma just two days ago."

"Trust me. I'll be ok. I might go for a run."

Vasia paused for moment while she regarded you. She had a solemn look in her eyes. "You have changed since the accident," she finally said.

"I'm ok," you repeated, somewhat more defensive than you meant to be.

"True, but that's the point. You've just come out of a coma, we had a marathon bout of lovemaking last night, you want to go for a run, and I don't think you got any sleep last night, but you don't look tired."

For a few seconds, you didn't know what to say and then, trying to laugh it off; "Are you really complaining about the sex?"

"No," Vasia said, smiling, blushing slightly.

"I promise, I'm ok," you repeated. "Now go to work,"

Vasia finally conceded with some reluctance to believe that you were indeed alright, and minutes later, she was out of the door and driving to work.

For a few moments, you leaned on the door, with your back to it. You took in the sudden quietness and realisation that you were alone for the first time in days.

Despite trying to reassure Vasia that you were fit and healthy, you wondered yourself if that was true. In fact, you felt refreshed and invigorated as if you were having the required eight hours sleep a night.

Never one to dwell on personal problems for long, you remembered the envelope in your pocket. You got it out, and after noticing the postmark was London, you felt a sinking feeling in the pit of your stomach.

With a finger, you slit the envelope open and took out a single A4 piece of paper folded in three places. You unfolded the paper. It was from IntelliTech. The first five words were: "We regret to inform you..."

With a mix of both frustration and apathy, you scrunched up the piece of paper into a ball and chucked it in the bin. You didn't need to read it all to know it basically said, "You didn't get the job."

"I didn't want it anyway." You said to the bin.

Trying not to let the rejection get to you, you looked

at the kitchen table. With breakfast now cold and abandoned, you sighed and started tidying up.

Afterwards you climbed the stairs to change into your running gear. Despite feeling down, you still felt the need to go for a run.

*

Minutes later dressed in red lycra top, blue shorts, and a pair of Asics trainers, you filled up your bottle with water. You switched on the running app on your smartphone to track your run and set the playlist to Foo Fighters Greatest Hits. In your humble opinion, anything by the Foo Fighters made for great running songs.

You headed out onto the Busway on a brilliant spring morning with the Sun shining high.

A little bit up the Busway, there is this gate that leads to a meadow. Beyond the meadow is a steep hill that you usually have to use all your willpower to sprint all the way up. Inevitably you more often than not stop to walk it. However, on this occasion, you sprinted up to the summit with the ease of Usain Bolt running 100 metres.

At the summit, there is a panoramic view of Luton with the M1 motorway to the east, fields that went on further than you can see to the south, and the residential and industrial estates to the west.

In the morning's spring sun, the view betrayed Luton's reputation as the second ugliest town in the United Kingdom. Perhaps your recent brush with death had changed your perception on things.

You took several photos of the view with your smartphone plus a selfie with the sun shining on the motorway disappearing over the horizon. "That's going straight on *Facebook.* #running selfie" you chuckled to yourself before you started heading back down the hill.

The plan was to take it easy and only jog four miles,

two miles up, and two miles back. Yet, when the app notified you that you were already at the two-mile mark, quicker than you expected, you were buzzing.

Not being a particularly natural runner, your personal best was nine and a half minutes per mile. You had just managed to run the last two miles in seventeen minutes and ten seconds. You are not going to stop now. The visit from the police and the rejection letter now a distant memory you carried on.

At the third mile mark, you were passing the entrance to Dog Kennel Walk in Dunstable. The app notified you, you had just run the last mile in eight minutes and twenty-nine seconds, a full minute off your personal best.

You were positively laughing at your achievement, and still, you carried on running, going faster and faster.

At the four-mile mark, you had long ago reached the end of the Busway and was passing a big supermarket in Houghton Regis. The app told you that you were now running at eight minutes and eleven seconds per mile.

People on the street saw you running hell for leather, but as the great *Phoebe* from *Friends* once implied, it's only for a second, and then you're gone.

You were passing the old Chequers pub when the running app whispered in your ear again; You had just completed five miles. The last mile, you had run in seven minutes and fifty seconds.

"Holy crap," You exclaimed to yourself.

You immediately slowed and came to a standstill.

After taking a swig of water from your bottle, you took your smartphone out of your shorts pocket to check the app was working correctly.

Unbelievably it was working.

"I don't understand." You whispered to yourself "How can I run this fast."

You weren't even out of breath either.

You put your hand to your head and inspected your fingers "I'm not sweating."

This last fact was very abnormal for you because in whatever physical activity you're doing, you easily sweat.

After a moment of deliberation, you tested something out.

Weeks ago, you had programmed some training runs onto your app, which would direct you like a Sat Nav would with a car.

These training runs increased in length to twenty-two miles, which you hoped you could do for your last training run before the marathon. You selected the twenty-two-mile circular route and noted on it you had already run five. With the course programmed into your smartphone, you set off again.

Continuing up Parkside Drive, you came to a lane that eventually led to Kestrel Way.

A short while later, you were running through a tunnel that ran underneath the M1 motorway.

Here a young lady walking, minding her business, wearing headphones, jumped and let out a little scream as you whizzed past her.

"Sorry!" You yelled over your shoulder, feeling guilty,

After the tunnel, you turned left and stepped onto a footpath that ran parallel to the motorway.

The footpath led to a corn field. You entered and ran around, following the public byway, and minutes later, entered another field.

Eventually, seven miles and forty-six minutes later, you were at the back of Toddington Service Station. Not stopping, you entered the service area on the Northbound side and crossed the car park. Annoyed drivers beeping their horns greeted you, and some were shouting profanities at you.

"Oi, Forrest Gump what the hell do you think you're doing?" One van driver yelled out of his window, who had to break suddenly

"Sorry. Can't stop." You yelled back over your shoulder.

"Numb nuts." The guy said, shaking his head.

You were so in the zone that you didn't take any notice of the insult. It didn't even occur to you how you managed to hear him.

You ran across the narrow footbridge over a busy M1 to the Southbound side. You barely took in the view of the motorway disappearing into the horizon, both north and south.

Without breaking a stride, you crossed the car park on the southbound side greeted by more car horns and angry curses, where you entered another field and carried on going.

You ran the last ten miles in sixty-five minutes, which you worked out was a speed of six and a half minutes per mile. A full three minutes off your personal best!

You entered your house two hours and thirty-three minutes after you had left. You felt you could have easily run more to complete a fall marathon. Hell, perhaps even an ultra-marathon or two. Hardly out of breath and with only a fine sweat on your forehead, you stretched and showered out of habit.

During the shower, you worked out that if you had carried on running to complete a marathon, you could have done it five minutes shy of three hours.

After the shower, you googled the record for the fastest time the London Marathon was run in. It was two hours and four minutes, so your time was hardly impressive compared to that. But considering a week ago, the best estimated time for me would have been five hours. This was mind-blowing. "I'm going to try better tomorrow." you quietly vowed to yourself.

Later, once you had sat down and calmed down from the buzzing euphoria of the run, your thoughts started turning solemn.

Thoughts such as how the hell had you ran that fast after being in a coma just two days ago? And how the hell had you run that far without feeling in the least bit exhausted? You were beginning to feel slightly troubled and thought maybe you should see a doctor. After some deliberation you decided to do just that and picked up the phone to make an appointment for the next day.

Chapter 14

That evening, Vasia's mum Hester, dad Rafa, and younger brother Wafiq were at yours for dinner.

The five of you were sitting at the dining table eating a roast dinner that Vasia and you had cooked together, with Wafiq and you discussing your recent job interview.

"How did it go?" Wafiq asked, pleasantly enough.

Wafiq was short but muscular and preferred to wear muscle vests. His long jet-black hair was slicked back with way too much gel.

When you first started dating Vasia, Wafiq, being the overprotective brother and a traditional Muslim, continuously tried to intimidate you out of the relationship. One of his signature moves was to out-stare you with those freaky dark eyes of his.

That was until Vasia, who was probably the only person Wafiq feared, had a quiet word with him.

Nowadays, Wafiq and you get on really well, and you even consider each other as best buds. You were so good in fact that, as typical men do, you would often just talk about putting the world to rights and shoot the breeze. Which was probably why the conversation turned the way it did.

"Yeah, it was ok as interviews go." you shrugged nonchalantly.

"Actually," Vasia piped up, "It probably didn't go too well, did it, darling?" Vasia emphasised the word 'darling' to show she was not impressed. You instantly looked sheepish.

"Why, what happened?" asked Hester.

"I may have told the interviewer he was a joke," you mumbled.

"What, why did you do that?" Rafa asked. He tried to feign shock but didn't quite succeed as he started chuckling.

"Well, he was asking all these daft questions, and then he asked me to tell him a joke. So, I said he was," you explained.

Laughing, Rafa asked, "What other questions did they ask?"

"Stupid ones," you answered instantly. "Like why are tennis balls fuzzy? And do I believe in ghosts?"

"Do you?" Wafiq asked.

"Do I what?" you asked, momentarily confused.

"Believe in ghosts?"

"Oh, God, don't start him on that," Vasia groaned.

I may have mentioned this before but after being together for so long Vasia knew what topics made you go off on a rant.

Vasia's groan was met with laughter from yourself and Vasia's family.

"At least they didn't ask you about aliens," Vasia said but the look on her face said she instantly regretted it.

"Well, I have said before that in this big massive universe of ours, with billions and billions of planets, it's only logical to assume that there must be alien life out there. I just don't believe that they have ever come here."

"Why do you think that?" Wafiq seemed to be genuinely interested, but he was relishing the resulting groan from Vasia too.

"Well," you started off amidst more laughter and groans, "If you think about it, for aliens to come here, they must be hundreds if not thousands of years more advanced than we are."

Take in the fact that we humans have only walked the moon once in the last fifty years, and we are only just talking about sending humans to Mars within the next ten years or so. We haven't even spoken about sending humans out of our solar system yet. If you look at our current rate of technological evolution, I don't think that will happen for another one to two hundred years yet.

Also, take in the fact about how fast we can go. Conventional rocket engines can travel 18,000 miles per hour, which means at current speeds, it would take about fifty-seven years to get to the edge of our solar system. Scientists are looking at an alternative form of propulsion using ion technology that, if we go ahead with, could mean we can travel up to 200,000 miles per hour. Now you might think that's fast, but that means it will still take five years just to get to the edge of our solar system.

Now, say far in the future we develop faster-than-light technology or as the scientific minds call it; 'FTL'" You actually used your fingers as quotation marks. "And for argument's sake, we use the warp drive scale in Star Trek, at Warp 1 it would take thirteen hours to get to the edge of our solar system. You might think that's fast, but if we try to travel to what we at the moment think is the nearest habitable planet, which is in the Proxima Centauri system, approximately four light-years away, at Warp 1 that would take four years to get there."

When you stopped for a breather you noticed that Vasia was sitting back in her chair, looking up towards the ceiling, exaggerating boredom. You wanted to stop but Wafiq was listening intently. You had a captive audience. Vasia's mother and father were just looking at you with blank looks.

"So, what's your point? Why don't you believe aliens have come here?" Wafiq asked and chuckled as Vasia groaned again.

"My point is, if we could develop FTL technology, bearing in mind our current rate of technological evolution, which I said before could be another one to two hundred years or more. And remember, when we eventually do have FTL technology, it will still take four years to get to the next habitable planet. So for aliens to come to visit us, it stands to reason that they are even faster than that and will be thousands of years more advanced than us. And if they are that advanced, why would they be interested in coming to visit us? I just don't believe they will."

"Don't you think they would be interested in coming to visit us if we develop FTL technology? Using your Star Trek analogy, couldn't they be watching and waiting for us to develop Warp Drive before they make First Contact with us?" Wafiq asked.

"Doubt it. If they were watching us, I reckon we would know it, with all our satellites and telescopes in space."

Vasia and her parents looked on with equal amounts of amusement and bemusement. As Wafiq and you continued to talk Vasia leaned over to her mum. "Do you think they will notice if we left the table?"

Hester answered with a roll of the eyes. "Do you want help clearing the table?" she asked, hopefully.

"Yes, please." Vasia responded gratefully

The two of them got up from the table and started clearing it while you and Wafiq carried on talking.

"But if they were thousands of years more advanced than us, maybe they would have developed a way to be invisible to us."

"I disagree," Wafiq said. "They might be able to cloak themselves."

And so, Wafiq and you continued to chew the fat about the unlikely possibilities of aliens and ghosts.

Somehow, as most conversations go when two men are just chatting, it inevitably turns to football and who would top the Premier League this season.

"Uh-humm I think I might join you two." Rafa immediately said getting up. He was more of a cricket man.

"Liverpool will win again this year." Wafiq uttered.

"No way." you yelled disgusted. You were surely loud enough for the whole neighbourhood to hear. "Arsenal are looking good for it. They're already second."

Also, politics and the latest current television trend entered the mix too

"It still blows my mind that he's an android." Wafiq uttered at one point.

*

Eventually, it was getting late, and Vasia's family had made their excuses and left.

You were standing at the sink doing the washing up while Vasia stood for a moment in the doorway to the kitchen, leaning on the doorframe, watching you. After a while, she came up behind you. She put her arms around you and laid her head on the top of your back.

"Thank you," she whispered.

"For what?"

"For putting up with my family this evening. I know it's not always easy for you," Vasia was referring to how strained the relationship used to be, between her and you and the rest of her family. It was ancient history now but was still at the forefront of your minds.

"Nonsense, I had fun. Wafiq and I get on really well now."

"Yeah," Vasia agreed. "Even if you two did bore the rest of us," she added jokingly.

Her left hand stroked the side of your leg and traced a line to your fly, where she fumbled for a second before undoing the zip.

"What on earth are you doing?" The question implied frustration, but the smile on your face implied you knew precisely what Vasia was doing and was more than happy for it to go ahead.

Vasia giggled as her hand slid into the opening and massaged your manhood.

"Stop it! I'm trying to do the washing up!"

Vasia just giggled again and carried on playing with your member, which was getting increasingly hard. To be honest, it had started growing in anticipation as soon as you knew that Vasia was watching you from the doorway.

Eventually, you could no longer concentrate on the washing up. Your hands still soapy, you turned away from the sink and kissed Vasia passionately on the mouth.

As she continued to massage your phallus, you planted small quick kisses and licked a line from her neck and shoulders. At the same time, you grabbed both her breasts and rubbed them with the heel of your hands.

With her free hand, Vasia traced a line up your stomach until she got to one of your nipples, and she played with it, knowing that this was one of your favourite erogenous zones.

Finished with her breasts for the moment, you undid the button on Vasia's jeans and unzipped the fly. Her jeans fell to the floor, revealing black cotton panties. you slid one of your hands into her panties, found the lips of her womanhood, and massaged it.

Vasia moaned with pleasure. She pulled at your t-shirt and tried to get it off you, but it was awkward.

Laughing, you stopped massaging Vasia's lady bits to slip your t-shirt off. Vasia followed suit and slipped her blouse off, revealing her curvy physique. She also took her black cotton bra off, exposing her ample breasts.

For a moment, the two of you stood admiring each other's bodies, with Vasia's eyes roving over your increasingly athletic physique.

"Sweetie, have you been working out?" she suddenly asked, puzzled.

You looked down at your own body. It did look like you were well on the way to developing a six-pack. As with not being able to sleep and the sudden speed you were running at earlier, this should be another thing for you to worry about. But not wanting to ruin the mood, there was only one thing on your mind right now. "It must be all the running I'm doing for the marathon." you shrugged nonchalantly.

You moved in on Vasia, first kissing her hungrily on the mouth, then her neck and left shoulder, and then moved down to her breasts, licking and playfully biting at each nipple. With your tongue, you traced a line from her breasts down the middle of her stomach to her cotton panties.

And that's where you made love right on the ceramic tiled kitchen floor. At one point you both climaxed but like some crazed animals you were still eager to carry on.

You somehow made your way to the living room with a brief dalliance in the hallway. You had penetrated Vasia from behind and had her against the door frame. You were both grunting and breathing heavily. Vasia could feel the size of your phallus in her anus. Eventhough it hurt a little it wasn't unpleasurable judging from the heavy groaning.

However, it wasn't long before you ended up on the sofa with Vasia straddling you.

Eventually your bodies glistening with sweat, Vasia and you both climaxed again screaming in unison. Although just like the other night, your screams were mostly out of the feeling you get when you're on the downward trajectory of a roller coaster.

Still straddling you, after several long moments, Vasia eventually said, "Not that I'm complaining, but where have you found the stamina to do that the second night on the trot?"

You tried to shrug indifferently. "I'm not sure."

Trying to start up the conversation they had that morning, Vasia said, "You have definitely changed since the coma. Are you sure you're ok?"

You opened your mouth to claim you were fine but paused wondering yourself if you really were fine.

Finally, feeling emotional, you admitted, "I don't know. Something strange has been happening to me, and I don't know what to do." Your voice hitched on the last few words,

Vasia pulled you in for a hug and said, "What's been happening?"

You told Vasia everything, starting from the first night you woke up from the coma when you thought you had dreamt that someone had died in the hospital, then when you walked to their room they actually did die. You included what happened at the pub the day before and the reason you ran out.

Between all that, you had had no sleep but was not feeling tired, there was the marathon lovemaking as Vasia put it. There was also the running and the itch you had to go for another. You left out the bit about feeling weird and dizzy while you were having sex. You thought that might hurt her feelings more than anything. Besides, you still enjoyed it. In terms of your body changing, there was the six pack that Vasia noticed plus you were sure all your grey hairs had disappeared. At that point, Vasia inspected your head to make sure. "Oh yeah." She said "You're no longer thinning on top, either."

Not sure if she was joking or not you were immediately defensive "I was not going bold." And then after a moment's thought "Was I?"

"So I have booked an appointment with my doctor to see what's going on." you finished saying.

"Do you want me to come with you?" Vasia asked

"No, you have to go to work. I'll be fine."

"Your face doesn't look too convinced."

You weren't sure how to respond to that but you didn't need too anyway. Reluctantly she accepted your answer anyway and carried on by saying. "Talking about work, we better get to bed. I have to be up in a few hours, and you have tired me out," she said, trying to put a humorous smile on but failing halfway.

You agreed. After detangling yourselves from the sofa, you climbed the stairs to bed leaving the clothes that scattered the whole ground floor to be picked up the next day.

*

An hour later, Vasia was in a deep sleep, but you were still wide-awake staring at the ceiling and listening to Vasia's snores. You had never noticed this before, but she sounded like Darth Vader.

Realising this was the new norm you quickly gave up trying to get to sleep and slipped out of bed. After relieving yourself in the bathroom, you changed into your running gear, grabbed a bottle of water from the kitchen, set the running app on your smartphone to track yourself, exited the house and went for another run.

*

As dawn was breaking, you were back. As you got to the front door, the running app announced that you had just run twenty-six miles.

"Fuck me," you cursed astounded.

You were hardly the Flash, but you were an hour faster than last time and had just beaten the world record by nearly 40 minutes, running a marathon in one hour and twenty-six minutes.

Chapter 15

Not long after coming back from your run, and you had you shower, you were making breakfast. You waited for Vasia to perform her morning prayers before you sat at the table.

"I take it, you didn't sleep again," she commented coming into the kitchen.

She kissed you good morning and sat down to eat.

"No, I went for another run," you explained.

Vasia looked thoughtful and then as if it had been playing on her mind for a while she asked. "What else have you been doing?"

"What do you mean?"

"Well, apart from rescuing damsels in distress, fucking my brains out, and going out for a run at crazy o'clock, what else have you been doing with yourself?"

Despite the situation, you chuckled to yourself. "I've been catching up on Sky Plus and Netflix." then looking serious, you added, "Although there are only so many episodes of The Walking Dead and Stranger Things."

"I suppose there is another advantage to not being able to sleep." Vasia said.

"How do you mean?"

"Well think about it, as you're looking for work, not having to sleep has given you the unique opportunity to look for night-time jobs. Not just daytime jobs. Or you could do both."

The look on your face suggested the thought hadn't occurred to you until now and at first you weren't keen on the idea.

"I don't think I will find many night time IT jobs," you said carefully. "But nighttime work usually pays better whatever it is," you added with more optimism.

"So, is it agreed you will look for night time jobs as well?" Vasia pushed on.

"Yes, I'll start today," you said a little defensively.

The stress of being out of work showed the strain it was putting on your relationship, if only for a split second.

"I'll have a look after I've been to the doctors," you promised.

Knowing when not to push it any further, Vasia finished eating her breakfast and got ready to go to work.

Just as she got to the front door to leave the house, you took her in your arms and kissed her passionately on the mouth. When you pulled away, Vasia was looking at you with playful inquisitiveness.

"Well, I can think of another advantage to me not getting tired," you answered Vasia's unspoken question. You had your trademark grin that you thought Vasia thought looked sexy. "Would you care to capitalise on it?"

Vasia, however, always thought that grin looked goofy. But knowing what it implied seemed to turn her on, anyway. It could have been the bulge she felt in your trousers when you pulled her in close.

You leaned in and started planting small kisses on Vasia's neck. Vasia let out a slight groan.

"We haven't got time. I've got to go to work," she bemoaned.

"They won't mind you being late for once. Blame it on the traffic," you said as you gently pushed Vasia up against the door. Still kissing her on the neck, you massaged her breasts.

Looking a bit flustered, Vasia took your head in both her hands and brought your face up level with hers. "I'm not kidding. I've got to go to work."

You answered by giving Vasia a long, deep kiss, which Vasia did not try to stop whatsoever.

She didn't attempt to stop you either when you pulled her trousers down to her ankles and kneeled to go down on her. The sudden shock of your tongue on her clit made Vasia gasp. You carried on going down on her, teasing her lady bud until Vasia was panting in excitement.

Before she could cum, you suddenly stood up.

Straight-faced; you said, "Well, you better get to work now. See ya." you turned to walk away.
Vasia's face was a picture. "You little shit." she started.

She grabbed you and turned you around. You started laughing.

Attempting to keep a stern face, she fumbled for the fly of your jeans, and after undoing it, your jeans fell to the floor.

She jumped and straddled you while you were still standing. No longer able to keep a stern look, Vasia started laughing. This caused you to start chuckling manically as well as you both slid to the floor.

And that's where you made love right in the hallway against the front door.

*

Sometime later, fully clothed again, Vasia left the house and went to work.

You left for the doctor's shortly after.

When you arrived at the doctor's surgery, you signed in at reception, and went to the waiting room. You didn't wait for long before the tannoy called you into her office.

Dr. Raleigh, whose nameplate on her desk said her first name was Rachel, had a perpetually bored expression, was in her late forties with long greying hair held in a tight bun.

For a doctor, she ironically looked unwell whenever you went to see her. She was stick thin, almost anorexic, with a slightly jaundiced complexion. Her long, thin nose was red on this occasion, indicating she may have a cold.

The gravelly sound of her voice proved this and that she had been suffering for a while.

"What can I do for you?" Dr. Raleigh asked, straight to the point.

"Well, this will sound strange, but I haven't slept since I was in the hospital, and I feel fine. Better than fine, in fact."

Dr. Raleigh stared at you for a few moments with a stony expression that was making you feel uncomfortable. She then turned to her computer screen, presumably to read your notes.

"You were in hospital three days ago, where you spent two days?"

The question sounded more like a statement of fact.

"Yes," you answered.

"You were in a coma?"

"Yes, for one night."

"After being knocked unconscious by a train explosion in the terrorist attacks in London on Monday?"

"That's right."

"So, you think you haven't been asleep for four nights."

Somehow you felt a little annoyed at her stating the obvious.

"I know I haven't," you answered. "Am I in any danger?"

"To begin with, I'm sure you must have had some sleep even if it's a quick sixty-minute nap here and there. Looking at you, you're awake and refreshed, not something you normally expect to see in someone who hasn't slept for five days."

"I know, that's the point, I'm sure I have not slept for five days, but I feel perfectly fine."

The doctor looked at me for a few moments. Her bored expression showed a hint of disbelief and questioned if I might be taking her for a ride.

"Ok," the doctor finally said. "How are your muscles? Are they aching?"

"No," was your quick answer.

"Any memory lapses or confusion?"

"No."

"Do you feel depressed?"

"No."

"Any history of depression in your family?"

"No."

And and this was your response to a load more questions until the doctor asked:

"Have you been suffering from any hallucinations?"

Your mouth opened to say no, but you stopped yourself when you remembered the night you rescued the woman from getting raped.

"I see," the doctor said, looking at you critically, taking your pause as confirmation for a yes.

"I don't know if it was a hallucination," you began. "It was more of an umm… a vision or umm… a prediction," you finished, feeling foolish.

"How do you mean?"

You explained the night you saw the woman getting raped. When you stopped, the doctor said nothing at first. She just stared dubiously at you.

Finally, it was you again who broke the silence saying, "Have you heard about this before?"

"I have," the doctor finally admitted, seeming to choose her words carefully. "If you really do have this problem with sleep like you say you do you will have to speak to a specialist who I will refer you to now and they will tell you more. However, I can say there has been research carried out on sleep deprivation. Going for lengthy periods of sleep can cause deficits in attention and memory. Sometimes if the lack of sleep goes on for too long, the memory loss can become permanent. After only twenty-four hours, some people can start experiencing hallucinations. There are other health problems, including the risk of diabetes, weight gain, even heart attacks, and death. Some people will experience micro-sleeps."

"What are micro-sleeps?"

"Micro-sleeps usually occur when a person is going through a prolonged period of sleep deprivation. It usually occurs when that person is performing a monotonous task such as driving or watching TV. It usually lasts a few seconds or a few minutes, and the person is not always aware of it, and almost always, their eyes are still open while it's happening. It's like going through a trance or having a blackout," the doctor defined. "Do you think your vision may have been a micro-sleep?"

The question sounded more like a suggestion.

"Maybe." you paused, unsure of yourself. "But it happened. Or it would have if I hadn't been there."

"The mind can play tricks on you even more so when you are sleep deprived. I reckon you were in some confused, tired state, you went out, witnessed this woman getting attacked, and had a feeling of deja vu because we all hear about women getting attacked in the media, don't we? Your brain, in its tired state, started misfiring electrons and made a link making you think you have seen it before."

"Maybe," you said again, even more, unsure of yourself.

"I'm sure that is what it was," the doctor said assertively.

Changing the topic slightly, you asked, "How long have I got before I experience any serious side effects?"

"As I said I will need to refer you to a specialist and they will tell you more. But, I would expect you to be feeling something by now. There are the hallucinations and the micro-sleeps that I have mentioned. Your emotions should start going all over the place now, so you will begin experiencing behavioural issues, mood swings, that kind of thing. Also, about now you should be experiencing bouts of

116

disorientation, sometimes it can be so bad you'll be delirious. Also, your blood pressure and heart will be affected as it's constantly working double-time to pump adrenaline around your body, which leads to the most serious side effect."

"What's that?" you asked with grim curiosity.

"Death," was Dr. Raleigh's curt reply, and then noticing the look of horror on my face, she hastily added, "However, that is very rare and only seen in a very minute percentage of cases."

When it looked like you relaxed a bit, she again added, "Although there are reports that a man in China died after going ten days without sleep."

"Ten days!" you echoed, feeling sick as you realised you had been awake for almost half that. Raleigh, nodding, said, "Yes, but as I have said very rare, and we have known people to go without sleep for longer than that."

"What is the known longest time for someone to stay awake?"

"I think the world record is about eighteen days set by a Peterborough lady in the 1970s. She was in a rocking chair competition."

"What happened to her after eighteen days?" you asked, your anxiety rising.

She seemed to give the question some thought as she studied your expression.

"She fell asleep. I presume. But I will have to check on that for you. However, there is another story I've heard of a man in America who stayed awake for eleven days. When he finally fell asleep, he slept for fourteen hours straight the first time, woke up at about nine in the morning, and fell asleep again at eight in the evening when he slept for another ten hours. He appeared to fully recover from his lack of sleep after less than a week with no long-term health problems. So, I'm optimistic that you will recover once you're able to go back to sleep."

You felt slightly better about yourself hearing these two accounts until you brought up the subject of the side effects you should feel now.

"Doc, you said my heart rate and blood pressure should be high, but I feel fine. In fact, I have been on a few runs," you said, omitting the length and time of my runs.

"Let's take a look and see shall we."

She took your heart rate with a stethoscope and took my blood pressure. When done, she returned to her desk and looked at you, slightly confused.

"Was my heart rate and blood pressure, ok?" you asked, concerned by her look.

"Yes, it's all normal," she admitted.

"That's good then."

The doctor got a notepad and pen out and started writing.

"What are you doing?" you asked.

She handed a prescription to me.

"I am prescribing you some Rameltoen. It will hopefully make you go to sleep. Take one tablet a day about thirty minutes before you plan to go to bed." Dr. Raleigh turned to her computer and brought up her calendar. "I will also book you in for another appointment to see me again after the weekend. Is the same time on Monday ok with you?"

"It is."

"Good, I will see you in three days. Hopefully, you would have gotten some sleep by then."

"What if I haven't, even with the meds?"

"If not, I will have to refer you to that specialist."

You were really hating that she was so blunt. You thanked the doctor and bid her goodbye. After getting the Ramelteon (which you would never actually take) from the pharmacy next door to the GP surgery, you went back home, where you spent most of the day on your desktop PC before Vasia came back home from work.

You had every intention to look for work, but you spent almost all that time procrastinating and googling sleep deprivation. Most of what you found the doctor had already confirmed

Chapter 16

A few minutes after five o'clock that evening, seconds before Vasia walked through the door; you had another one of your visions as you would later come to know them as. It came without warning while you were still internet surfing. One second you were sitting at your computer. The next, you were standing on the hard shoulder of the southbound side of the M1 at junction 11.

Cars, vans, and lorries were whizzing noisily past you in the late evening sun. One wide-load truck angrily beeped at you as it went past because you were standing too close to the rumble strip.

You stepped back in time, getting a face full of wind and grit.

Seconds after the lorry went past; you were looking at the incoming traffic in time to see the passenger side front tyre of a red Vauxhall Astra blow out.

Even over the din of the motorway traffic, it was deafening. It sounded like a gunshot. As you watched, the driver, a middle-aged, chestnut greying hair, white male fought to wrestle control of his car. The blond-haired middle-aged female in the passenger seat looked like she was having a panic attack.

The driver made a valiant effort to keep control, the car veered halfway into the second lane, almost colliding with the white Ford, who at the last minute veered into the third lane. The driver of the car in the third lane had nearly the same quick reflexes and tried to swerve out of the way.

The third driver didn't have the same luck as the other two. He collided with the central reservation. In a shower of sparks, and an almighty screeching noise made by high speed metal colliding with stationary metal, the driver's side completely crumpled under the impact. He was going at such a speed that at first, he didn't stop. He couldn't. Instead, the front end of the car got pushed up on top of the central reservation. It slid across it until it lost balance and came off onto the third lane of the northbound side in front of oncoming traffic.

The female in a black Range Rover travelling in that lane had barely time to register the car appearing in her vision, but she veered out of the way just in time. Unfortunately, she overcompensated on her steering, flipping her vehicle over on its side. Her speed forced the 4x4 to roll multiple times until she slammed into the right side of a fully-loaded car transporter.

In shock, the driver of the car transporter instinctively applied the brakes, but the Range Rover was caught in its tyres, and the carrier jackknifed. The back end of the transporter came out. It collided with the central reservation, getting stuck on it and sent showers of sparks all over the place.

The central reservation was slowing the jackknifed lorry down, but just before he came to a stop, the reservation buckled under the pressure as if it was just cardboard. The shock of the impact broke the straps that were holding the new Nissans sitting on the car transporter. As the transporter came to a stop, they rolled forward and one fell off onto its back on the southbound side of the motorway, into the path of a green BMW. The driver of the BMW had already seen what was going up ahead, and he was already slowing down. He stopped just short of a Nissan falling in front of him.

During this confusion, the Red Astra, whose tyre blew out and had caused this tragic chain of events, veered onto the hard shoulder, missing you by a whisker. You dived out of the way just in time. It turned a third and then a fourth time, its tyres making skid marks on the road surface.

Eventually, the car came to a safe stop on the hard shoulder. Immediately the driver, a middle-aged man in a red sports coat, and his female passenger got out of the car to inspect the damage. They stood mouths agape as they saw the carnage that they had caused.

Traffic on both sides came to a stop as the multi-car accident more or less blocked both sides.

Not all drivers were paying attention to the slowing traffic. Further up the southbound side of the motorway, a BP Fuel lorry was travelling up the middle lane at speed. Two people were inside the cab; the passenger, a spiky-haired male in his early twenties, still showing the remnants of adolescent acne, was asleep snoring with his mouth wide open. The driver, a bearded, obese male in his late forties, looked like he was about to join his mate in the land of slumber.

The radio was on, and the DJ was talking to some random celebrity about the latest love of their life. Having had enough of the conversation, the driver changed the channel and flicked through the radio stations with one disinterested eye on the road.

A Vauxhall Movano truck carrying scaffolding urgently beeped at him for getting too close up his backside and suddenly brought the driver's attention back to the road.

Cursing, the lorry driver applied the brakes and the wheels immediately locked with an awful screeching sound as he skidded, sending showers of sparks and the smell of burning rubber into the air.

It was too late. He slammed into the back of the van, violently nudging it forward. The van swerved from lane to lane, trying to gallantly gain control and avoid the slowing traffic.

Meanwhile, the shock of the collision caused the lorry to swerve and jackknife. As the fuel tank swung out to the left, it hit a red Mini, pushing it onto the hard shoulder over the barrier and into a ditch where it ended upside down on its roof.

122

Despite the van driver's efforts, he lost control as the last swerve was too tight, toppling him over onto his side and spilling all the scaffolding onto the motorway in an almighty cacophony of noise. One pole pierced the back window of a VW Beetle and missed the driver by mere millimetres.

With an awful groaning noise, the weight of the tank and the sheer momentum caused the cab to topple to the floor, and the tank fell onto its side. With an immense shrieking noise of asphalt on metal, in a shower of sparks, the tank slid down the motorway. It knocked several cars out of the way as if they were Lego bricks until it hit the Movano van. The unlucky driver who was trying to climb out the now vertical driver's door had no chance to escape as he watched with horror the tank barreling down on him.

The force of the impact sent scaffolding flying into the air.

One pole pierced the side of the tank, and fuel trickled out.

Most of the other poles fell harmlessly to the floor apart from one.

Whistling through the air like a spear, it flew straight for Red Astra guy.

Before Red Astra guy knew what was happening, the scaffolding pierced his face, decapitating him. The wife screamed as his lifeless body fell to the floor.

Seconds later, the BP tanker exploded, enveloping the traffic and people around in flames. With no time to register the impending pain, they immediately turned to blackened dead husks.

With a bump, you found yourself back at your computer console.

Wasting no time, in one swift movement, you leaped out of your seat, sprinted up the hallway and yanked the front door open where Vasia happened to be standing in the process of trying to find her keys to open it.

For some reason, you paid no attention and ran straight past her.

"Where the hell are you going?" Vasia shouted after your fast retreating back as you brushing past her caused her to drop her keys.

Not bothering to answer, you just carried on running and was soon around the corner and out of sight.

Before you were out of earshot, you could hear her cursing some more and questioning your sanity before she went into the house, slamming the door shut behind her.

With no clear thought of where you were actually going, you sprinted past rows of houses. You crossed four lanes of heavy traffic on the Dunstable Road with the sounds of breaking tyres, honking horns, and even a few curses of profanity from some drivers.
You ignored all this and ran up the slip road towards the motorway dodging and weaving the oncoming traffic.

At one point, you even jumped over a silver Astra that had no chance of stopping. It wouldn't cross your mind until later to wonder how you had done it.

As you got to the top of the slip road, you could hear that the events of the traffic accident were already unfolding. When you ran entirely onto the motorway, you were just in time to see the BP Lorry breaking and making that awful screeching sound.

You were pretty sure you knew what would happen next, so not bothering to stop, you turned in the direction of Red Astra couple and started towards them.

Running, focused on one thing you were vaguely aware of the events from your vision unfolding behind you as if it was in slow motion.

First, the lorry collided into the back of the van, which caused it to swerve multiple times and topple over, spilling the scaffolding all over the road in a great cacophony of noise.

Seconds before that came the horrible screeching and groaning noise that signaled the start of the lorry jackknifing and then the sound of metal on metal as it collided with the toppled van.

Then there was the horrible whistling noise as one pole came flying.

You got to Red Astra man.

You hadn't had a clear thought in your head from the moment you ran out of the house which is why you stupidly stood in front of the couple facing the oncoming scaffolding.

The Red Astra couple, had up to this point been staring at the unfolding carnage with dumbfounded slack-jawed expressions. Their expressions slowly turned to confusion when you suddenly appeared in front of them. Then they turned to surprise and shock. This was because the scaffolding hit you square in the stomach.

The sheer force of the collision caused the wind to be knocked out of you. You doubled over and fell to your knees. For a few moments, the pain was excruciating. You couldn't breathe. It felt like you had gone ten rounds with *Anthony Joshua*. The scaffolding pole fell harmlessly to the floor.

"My God, are you ok?" asked Red Astra woman from behind, her voice full of shock and concern.

You got to your feet, still clenching your stomach. The pain was still there, but it was subsiding quickly. You lifted your top to inspect the damage, and pain quickly turned into bewilderment. There was definitely some internal bleeding judging by the nice little black and green bruise covering half your washboard abs. But as you were looking, it was rapidly disappearing.

"Are you ok, son?" Red Astra man asked, echoing his wife's shock and concern.

The man's question broke you out of your reverie and back to the real world.

Remembering the events from your vision, you suddenly realised what would happen next.

"It will explode," was your answer. You pulled my top down on a now blemish-free stomach.

"What?" asked the bewildered Red Astra couple.

Everything had gone deadly quiet, or that was how you remembered it later. Panic slowly settled in as you watched people climbing out of the carnage. Those that were uninjured, or at least less injured than others, were helping the more severely injured out of various wreaks. Some were wandering around, dazed and confused. Others were taking pictures with their smartphones. One or two were actually taking selfies with the wreaks behind them. Despite the rising panic inside you, you felt a moment of disgust toward those two.

"It will explode," you repeated several times more quietly to yourself.

For what seemed like an eternity, you felt paralysed. Not sure what to do but certain that the lorry would explode any second now.

The Red Astra lady placing an uncertain, hopefully, comforting hand on my arm broke you out of your paralysis.

Facing the couple for the first time, you shouted at them, "Run. It's about to explode."

The couple just stood there looking at you gormlessly.

Shaking your head you didn't bother waiting for them to move. You turned and started running towards the carnage. As you ran, you shouted at people to head for safety. Most people were on the ball, and taking your advice, they started running for safety. A few, like the Red Astra Couple and especially those taking selfies, just looked at you with dumb expressions. Whether or not it was out of shock, you didn't know.

As you neared the lorry, you could plainly see the leaking fuel.

Just in front of the leak, a black mini was on its side with a young couple inside. As the car had finished ending up on the driver's side, the driver was lying in an awkward heap on the driver's door, unconscious with a massive gash on his head. The passenger, a brown-haired female, was trying to climb up out of the passenger door.

You had to jump over the bonnet of a Vauxhall Astra in American cop movie style to get to the Mini and climbed up the Ford Focus that it had finished resting against.

From here, you quickly helped the woman out of the Mini and down the side of the Focus. After telling her to get a safe distance away, you turned your attention to the unconscious man. Precariously you laid on your front on the side of the mini.

"Hey," you called to the unconscious man. "Are you awake?"

The man did not answer, and his eyes did not open. Despite that, you could tell he was still alive. You could just make out that his chest was moving up and down, and where the man's head was partially resting on the broken glass of the driver's door, it was fogged up. Proof that he was breathing.

You looked up at the lorry and the leaking fuel.

You had a flashback to the train accident, to the moment you were saving the kids before it exploded. Tempted to turn and run then. It was a similar feeling now. You are not afraid to admit that leaving the unconscious man, briefly flashed through your mind. You didn't know the guy. You would not be too upset by his death.

Instead, shaking your head as if to get rid of the idea, you reached through the passenger door.

You got hold of the man by the collar of his coat and lifted him out of the car. The ease you did it with, you wouldn't think to question until later.

"To hell with not moving anyone in case they have a broken spine," you said to the unconscious man. "Better living with a broken spine than dying in a ball of fire."

Once out of the car, you put the guy over your shoulder, in a fireman lift, jumped down from the Ford Focus, and ran to where the female passenger was safely waiting on the exit slip road. Two paramedics had just arrived on the scene. As they saw to the unconscious man, you turned back to face the carnage.

In that law of tired cliches, the lorry should have exploded after you had just got away from it in the nick of time.

"Why hasn't it exploded yet?" you wondered quietly to yourself.

Then you heard a call for help from your right. You turned and saw between the lorry and the barrier on the edge of the road, a late twenty-something, tired but attractive looking, black woman with her hair up in a messy bun. She was climbing over the barrier from the ditch of the side of the road. She was having an awkward time of it, because at the same time she was carrying what looked like a newborn baby girl in her arms, wrapped up in a pink blanket.

A flashback recalled the red Mini hit by the jackknifing fuel lorry, pushed onto the hard shoulder, and over the barrier. These must be the people from that car.

"Shit." You cursed to yourself and well aware that the truck was still going to explode any second now, you headed towards the woman and her baby. The woman was limping. In the best-case scenario, she had severely strained her left foot. She staggered and almost fell, but you got to her in time.

"Here let me help carry your baby." You offered

"Thank you." The woman gratefully accepted.

Carrying the baby in one arm and supporting the woman with the other, the three of you, as quick as the lady could go on her dodgy foot could go headed back to the relative safety of the slip road.

You had only got a few feet when you both heard a weird whooshing, whistling noise. You looked back at the lorry. The leaking fuel had caught alight, and it appeared the tank was absorbing the flames.

You reacted first and roughly shoved the woman back over the barrier and down into the ditch. You intended to follow behind her, aiming to cover them all from the impending explosion.

Before you could get safely over the barrier, the tanker exploded into a small ferocious mushroom cloud of fire sending glass, metal, and tarmac in all directions. Instinctively, you crouched to the floor, using your body to protect the baby from the remorseless, roaring fire that enveloped you.

For a few moments, your brain couldn't comprehend you were sitting in the middle of a ball of fire. Looking back at it, you can't recall feeling any pain at first.

Despite the heat, you felt a cold tingly feeling almost like pins and needles, and as the smell of burning meat reached your nose, you realised your skin was peeling away. More out of shock, you started screaming.

It wasn't until the fire subsided, and the air hit you, that you felt agonizing, vomit producing, faint inducing pain. The sound you heard gives you nightmares to this day. Imagine the noise you make cracking your knuckles. Now imagine that a thousandfold all over your body.

You looked down at your free hand.

"Oh my God," you moaned to yourself.

Fourth-degree burns covered your hand and what you could see of your arm. It resembled an overcooked, blackened pork chop.

It took you a few moments to realise though, that as you were looking, your hand and arm were healing. Staggered and dazed are too little to describe how you were feeling as you saw with your own eyes pink flesh quickly appearing.

After a while, the cracking knuckles sound stopped. The pain disappeared too.

You stood up and looked down at yourself. Your clothes were shredded and hanging off your body. And you were so black and sooty that a *Mary Poppins* chimney sweep would be proud. Apart from all that though you were blemish-free.

The baby girl you had protected, and was still holding in your arms was also burn and blemish-free. Surreally she was fast asleep with her thumb in her mouth.

Before you heard the shocked gasp, you were already beginning to feel a mix of panic, fear, and disbelief take over you. "What the hell is happening to me?" you ask yourself quietly

You looked up wide-eyed. Equally wide-eyed was the woman you had pushed into the ditch standing up staring at you. She must have seen you healing.

"Wh... wh... what are you?" the woman stammered in fear.

"I don't know," you answered quietly with an equal amount of fear.

Before you could finish, though, the woman rushed to grab her baby off you.

"Give me my baby," the woman said, crying.

"She's ok," you tried to reassure handing her child over.

"Please, give me my baby," the woman repeated.

The woman immediately ran off toward the paramedics and the crowd of people now standing on the slip road. All of them were staring at you, slack-jawed. Some had their mobile phones out videoing the scene.

"Shit," you quietly whispered to yourself.

Fear fully taking over, you started looking for a way to disappear quickly.

Towards the crowd on the slip road was not an option.

Going in the opposite direction was also not an option. There were people with their vehicles stopped by the accident in that direction. Keeping a safe distance, some of them were out of their vehicles with the odd few taking pictures or recording videos with their smartphones as well.

There was only one other way. With one hand on the barrier, you leaped over, jumped the ditch, and disappeared through the bushes.

On the other side, you came across an eight-foot-high chain-link fence, which you scaled up in quick succession and jumped to the ground on the other side.

In a kneeling crouch, you quickly took stock of your surroundings. It looked like you were in a spacious playfield of a school that was empty now, as the children had finished school for the week and had long gone home.

Hearing a commotion from behind, you could tell the people from the motorway were gathering at the barrier, trying to see where you had gone. Wasting no more time, you sprinted across the field. It was easily the same size as two or three football pitches, but you reached the other end within seconds. You vaulted over the gate on that side, sprinted across a busy road amidst the sounds of brakes screeching and drivers cursing at you again, and headed for home.

A few minutes later, you burst through the front door of your house, making Vasia jump out of her skin.

She was still peeved off that you had done a runner. The entire thing had only been twenty minutes give or take.

"Where the hell have you been?" She started but then she noticed the scared look on your soot stained face and the state of your clothes.

"What happened?" she asked with a growing mix of weariness and concern.

You told Vasia the whole story while she just stood there, mouth agape. When you started explaining the excruciating pain of being in the middle of the fire from the exploding lorry, you broke down crying and couldn't go any further.

Vasia put her arm around you to console you. She would have disbelieved you if it wasn't for the BBC breaking news story that suddenly started on the television.

Huw Edwards' dulcet Welsh voice announcing a tragic accident on the M1 snapped you out of your emotional mood, and you both looked up at the TV in silence. Suited as usual and sat at the news desk, he described the accident. "As tragic as it was, there are no fatalities yet, just one man who was in a critical but stable condition." He added.

You assumed this was the same man you had pulled out of the Mini.

The news anchor carried on "The reason why there are no fatalities, by all accounts, could be attributed to the actions of one man. He is described only as being in his early thirties, athletic build, and brown hair. This man, even though he has done nothing wrong, he is of great importance to the police."

The reason you were of great importance to the police became quickly apparent.

The screen cut to a very grainy video. It was the moment the truck exploded and the ball of flames enveloping you. The video was so pixelated and was only looking at you from behind that to a stranger you couldn't tell it was you. But you and Vasia knew.

Vasia let out a little scream and put her hands over her mouth when she saw the flames cover you. When the fire receded, although grainy, the video very clearly showed the man was burnt all over his body, but in a matter of seconds, he healed.

At that point, the video stopped, and Huw Edwards said there was some mobile phone footage too.

"Oh no," You apprehensively said to yourself, when the television screen cut to a video from a mobile phone. This one was taken by someone standing on the slip road, where the paramedics had been. It picked up right after the explosion and from the moment you had healed. It showed the mother of the baby you had saved, grabbing the baby out of your arms and running away towards the direction of the person taking the video and then disappearing behind the camera.

The Welsh newscaster went on to point out "This woman is clealy in a state of inconsolable panic and we understand is being given medication to help calm her down. The police have said she will hopefully be calm enough to talk to and help identify this mysterious man."

You gulped uneasily at that last bit.

It seems fortunate now your smoky soot-stained face tattered clothing made it difficult to identify you. But what was clear to the average viewer this person was scared. The video finished with the man leaping over the barrier and disappearing into the bushes.

The screen cut to another brief video taken from another mobile phone. This one was a lot shakier at first. The videographer was running towards the spot in the bushes that you had disappeared into. The video stabilised enough only to capture the back of the man who was already a substantial distance away, running with the speed of a cheetah, across a school field. As the video ended, you could just make out the man jumping over the gate on the other side of the field, and then he was gone.

The screen cut back to Huw Edwards in the newsroom and was asking the public to offer any information they may have. Vasia walked over to the TV and switched it off, cutting Huw off in mid-sentence.

A look of apparent concern, wordlessly she turned to you. All you could do was repeat what you asked yourself earlier: "What is happening to me?"

Chapter 17

Approximately thirty minutes after the news bulletin had gone out, Detective Stone and FBI Special Liaison Officer Agent Haider were sitting at their desks in an open plan, well lit, air-conditioned office on the third floor of Scotland Yard.

Despite being six o'clock in the early evening, the office was a gentle buzz of activity as detectives went about their business.

Stone was talking on the phone to his wife and his five-year-old daughter. He had adopted a softer tone to his voice as he asked if she had been a good girl at school today.

While that was happening, Haider's computer gently pinged to announce that someone wanted to instant message with him.

He saw it was Terry from Cyber Forensics and let out a little groan. Terry wasn't the most exciting person to converse with, especially as it was nearing the end of Stone and Haider's shift. The subject heading piqued his interest though; "M1 guy, is this your man?"

Haider clicked on the message and revealed a photo with the description "A satellite image taken of the moment after the truck exploded."

The satellite image, a hundred times zoomed, was a bird's-eye view of the accident on the motorway. You could see all the people on the slip road, the cars involved in the accident and who had stopped because of the accident. There was also the burning wreckage of a lorry. Metres away from the burning lorry was the figure of a man crouching down as if he was protecting something. He was looking up towards the sky. It seemed like he was screaming in pain.

Although the image was the byproduct of a marvel of human technological achievement, it wasn't fantastic. The guy's face was blurry. Despite that, Haider instantly recognised him.

He had only been looking at the photo for a few seconds when Terry sent another instant message: "So Haider, is this your guy?"

Stone was coming off the phone, saying his love you's and goodbye's.

When he put the receiver down, Haider waved him to come around to his side.

Stone did, and when he saw the photo, his eyes widened. "Could he clear the image up a little bit?"

Haider asked Terry the question and quickly got a reply. "Let me see what I can do. I'll let you know first thing tomorrow morning."

*

A few hours later, after Vasia and you had had a long, long discussion about what was happening. why it was happening, and even more importantly; how, the two of you were in bed. You were both naked. Vasia, her body still glistening with sweat, asleep on her side, was cuddling up to you with one hand on my chest.

Apparently the events a few hours before wasn't a good enough excuse to quell your new found sexual appetite.

You, of course, could not sleep. You were staring up at the ceiling, deep in thought, mentally processing the events of the day.

It was while you were deep in thought when you suddenly found yourself somewhere else. One moment you were lying in bed, the next you were standing on the platform of Green Park Underground Station.

You were wondering if you were having another vision, but it felt kind of different. Maybe because the platform was void of any people apart from yourself and, at first, void of any noise. You never knew the underground to be so quiet.

Unexpectedly a familiar screeching broke through the quietness and you felt the familiar wind of air coming up from the tunnel. A train was coming. Sure enough, a train soon came rumbling out of the tunnel and slowly came to a stop at the station.

As it was slowing, you noticed that there were no people on the train.

That was until the doors directly opposite you opened to reveal an elderly grey-haired, bearded black man in tribal clothing holding a wooden staff.

"Eraaf?" You exclaimed.

The, Xuholo tribesman leaned out of the carriage and whispered in your ear, "Come find me and all will be clear,"

Before you could question him on that, Eraaf held out his wooden staff, which for some inexplicable reason was glowing orange, and he lightly touched your head with the top end.

There was a brilliant, blinding flash of light, and you found yourself back in bed. You sat bolt up in bed, disturbing Vasia out of her sleep.

"What the fuck?" she sleepily cursed.

"I know what to do," you exclaimed excitedly.

"Yeah? What?"

"I've got to go to Africa!" you announced a trifle excited.

Still sleepy, Vasia's response was, "Yeah, yeah, yeah, go back to sleep, we'll discuss it in the morning." And she rolled over on her other side and went back to sleep.

Unperturbed by Vasia's response, you immediately got out of bed, put some clothes on, and went downstairs. You switched on the computer where you stayed till morning, trying to figure out how exactly you were going to get to Africa.

Chapter 18

Morning came. Vasia had now been up for an hour, and you were at the kitchen table where you were both now crowded round your laptop on a travel comparison website.

"Do you even know where in Africa?" Vasia was asking incredulously.

"Left of Sudan, I think," was your smart reply, and then thinking better of it, you added, "I remember Ermee saying it was somewhere on the borders between Sudan, Chad, and Libya."

"That is still a sizeable area to cover."

"I remember her saying something like Volta. I have done a quick Google search, and that place exists."

Still not convinced, Vasia asked, "And how do you think you will get there?"

"I've had a look, and if we leave this afternoon, we can fly from Heathrow to Khartoum, it's twenty-seven hours with a nineteen hour stop in Cairo, but we'll be able to do it."

"And how are you going to get from Khartoum to this Volta place?"

"We'll hire a car."

Vasia had a quick look on the laptop before she said, "You said this place is on the borders of Chad, Sudan, and Libya. From Khartoum to the border, it's almost 800 miles, so that will take about twelve hours, and that's without breaks."

"You realise I don't sleep anymore?" was your quick reply. "I don't need breaks."

"You realise it's mostly across the desert?" was Vasia's equally quick and exacerbated reply.

"So, I don't sweat." you shrugged, feigning calm. "But we'll take plenty of water."

"What about your doctor's appointment on Monday?" Vasia asked.

"I'll reschedule. Besides, I think my doctor can't help me with what I have."

Realising she was fighting a losing battle, Vasia then asked, "And what about your marathon?"

"That's not until next Sunday?"

"Twenty-seven-hour flight there and twenty-seven-hour flight back, that's fifty-two hours, add on the twenty-four-hour (plus breaks) round trip by car, then you have to find these people. You will not have as much time as you think you will have before you need to be back."

"We'll make it?"

"And what's this talk of we?" Seeing confusion spread on your face, Vasia carried on, "I'm not going. I can't. One of us has to work and pay for this little excursion."

Slightly deflated, you said, "Well, I was hoping you would come, but I could do it by myself. I am a big ugly man, after all." You tried to smile at the last comment to show it was a joke, Admittedly it was a weak one, and Vasia was not laughing.

*

So, despite Vasia's best intentions to dissuade you, you were at Heathrow Airport that evening, after Vasia had begrudgingly given you a lift there. Despite not being happy with the situation, Vasia still kissed you at the security gates with a little tear in her eye.

"Don't worry. I will be back," you reassured her.

"Just don't get into any trouble."

Now, you were standing in line to get on the plane for Cairo, waiting to show your ticket and passport to the desk clerk.

If you hadn't been so preoccupied, you would have noticed that you were being watched.

Detective Stone and Special Agent Haider had been on their way to yours and were actually driving up to your door when they noticed you and Vasia leaving the house. Obviously, you were going somewhere with a rucksack on your back. So, they were intrigued and decided to follow you.

Now they were watching you from the other side of the concourse. They were joined by a third guy. He was middle-aged, athletic build, shaved head and his chiseled face was covered with at least 3 days growth.

As you stood in the queue to embark the plane this third man came up and casually joined the queue with only a few people between you. It was clear his intention was to tail you to wherever you were going. For now, at least you were totally oblivious.

.

*

The EgyptAir flight to Cairo was just under five hours, and you passed the time by watching Netflix on your smartphone. One movie was the *Bruce Willis* classic, *Unbreakable*.
You usually loved watching superhero movies. However, Willis' character's struggle to come to terms with his powers caused you to muse about your own situation.

So far, you know you can run fast (not Flash fast) but quick, nonetheless. You don't need to sleep. There are the visions as well.

'If I practiced and honed my skills, I might be able to get next week's lottery numbers,' you thought with a smile, stroking your chin.

The smile quickly faded when you had a flashback to yesterday's traffic accident, and it caused you to recall how the fire from the exploding lorry engulfed you. The pain that had followed was more than excruciating. So, you can get hurt, which was not great for a superhero. However, you can heal very quickly you reminded yourself.

'There's another thing that a superhero can do that I can't,' you thought, and that was fight. You had not thrown a punch in anger since you were a school boy.

You were no coward, but when it came to confrontation, you preferred to talk your way out of it rather than use your fists. You more of a lover than a fighter. Then you remembered the other night when you rescued the lady from getting raped. Granted, you had a pool cue and had taken the potential rapists by surprise, and you were running on adrenaline. But despite all that, you had no idea how to fight.

You came out of your reverie and noticed that *Unbreakable* had now finished. You were watching an episode of *Daredevil*. It was the episode where Murdoch was figuring out designs for his superhero suit.

"I will need to get some kind of disguise." you admitted quietly to yourself recalling the motorway accident again and how everybody seemed to have a smartphone were videoing you

Chapter 19

After Vasia dropped you off at the airport, she had every intention to leave as quickly as possible, but on her way out, she spotted a coffee shop.

"Vasia," She said to herself. "No self-respecting woman would say no to a good coffee."

So, she didn't. After paying for and collecting her Americano, she sat at one booth overlooking the concourse.

Taking a sip now and then, she was absent-mindedly watching people busily going about their business. She was simultaneously lost in thought about you and the situation you two now found yourselves in.

She was really concerned about you. At the start of the week, you were in hospital in a coma. Now you were on a flight to God knows where in Africa to search for a tribe who might help you with whatever was going on with you.

She knew it upset you last night after the whole engulfed in flames thing. That was freaking the hell out of her as well. She could have lost her husband. The love of her life. That she didn't because you healed didn't make her feel any better.

"What was with all these new powers of Simon's?" Vasia was thinking *"And was this extra stamina one of these new powers."*

Thoughts of your extra stamina naturally turned to the quantity of lovemaking you two had been doing lately. Vasia usually thought of herself as a sensual, sexual woman, and the two of you shared that rare chemistry where you both enjoyed each other both physically and spiritually. But boy! The last few nights were something else.

After a few moments, she had to mentally stop herself from thinking about your antics when she realised she was turning herself on. Having to cross her legs to subdue the throbbing and not able to stop herself from blushing, she glanced around at the people in the coffee shop. She felt a pang of guilt as if they knew what she was thinking and would judge her on it.

'It is probably for the better he has gone for a week.' Vasia thought to herself. Going at it for the last few days had made her sore. So, it would give her a chance to recover.

Something out of the corner of her eye caught her attention and her recent thoughts were momentarily forgotten.

Through the crowds of people, it took her a few seconds to catch what it was.

On the far side of the concourse amongst people sitting in one of the departure lounges were the two detectives, Stone and (Special Agent) Haider. They were both leaning up against a concrete pylon. They were talking to each other about something. But what made Vasia's hair stand on end was that they were both intently watching her. 'What are they doing watching me?' she quietly wondered to herself. Many paranoid things came to mind. Mostly to do with you and recent events.

She didn't think they saw she noticed them watching her. So trying to remain calm, she purposefully drank the rest of her coffee in an exaggerated slow fashion.

Afterwards, she picked up her jacket and handbag. Still trying to remain calm, she left the coffee shop and made her way out of the airport to where she had parked the car.

With the size of Heathrow Airport in mind and the crowds of people she had to walk through or sidestep, it took a very long ten minutes to get there. Through all that time, she had a distinct feeling that Stone and Haider were following her.

After paying at the parking terminal, she reached the car. Looking at the window, she thought she saw a reflection of Stone and Haider. She spun around, but they weren't there.

Slowly increasing to "freak out", she fumbled for her car key. Eventually, she had it and immediately unlocked the car and got in.

Paranoia taking over she locked the doors before she switched on the engine and drove out of the car park.

Traffic was good today, so within minutes she was merging onto the M4 motorway.

Every few seconds, she looked through her rearview mirror, expecting to see someone following.

For a while, she noticed nothing suspicious and started to feel a little better thinking that she wasn't being followed. That was until she indicated and maneuvered into the lane to merge onto the M25 heading north. With most of her attention on the road ahead, she thought she saw the flash of a black BMW suddenly coming into her lane a few cars behind.

"Shit." Vasia quietly cursed to herself. Trying to keep one eye on the traffic in front and another eye on the traffic behind her, she was getting increasingly anxious.

It took all her willpower not to beep at the cars in front who had all slowed down to a thirty mile per hour crawl. As is usually the case with the amount of congested traffic trying to all merge onto the London orbital motorway.

She finally made it onto the M25, and traffic became clearer so she could speed up a bit. For a while, though, she stayed in the first lane watching out for the black BMW. She was sure it was still three cars behind her.

She manoeuvred into the second lane.

The black BMW manoeuvred into the second lane too.

"Shit." Vasia cursed again. She was sweating with anxiety.

She manoeuvred into the third lane.

The Black BMW manoeuvred into the third too.

"No, no, no." She started repeating to herself desperately.

Trying to control her breathing, she started thinking of a way she could get out of this situation.

She purposely manoeuvred back into the first lane and slowed down slightly, trying to think. With her eight year old Astra, there was no chance in hell she could out speed and out maneuver the BMW.

For a while, she stayed at a steady sixty miles per hour while traffic zoomed past her. All the while, the BMW tried to stealthily stay behind, keeping at least three cars in between. It wasn't any easy task, considering it seemed everyone else wanted to drive at the limit.

Signs were pointing out that she was getting closer to the junction for the M1 and home.

As she was about to pass Junction 20 for Aylesbury and Hemel Hempstead, she changed her mind and suddenly veered onto the slip road. The tires screeched in protest. The whole car vibrated noisily as it went over the rumble strip. Bits of asphalt bounced up, hitting the undercarriage of the car. The BMW at the last possible moment came off, too, and continued to follow Vasia.

She intended to take the scenic route home and hopefully lose the BMW in the twists and turns of the country roads.

As soon as she got around one bend, she immediately put the car in fifth gear and floored it. The Astra launched off at speed. By the time she was going around another bend, the BMW was just coming round the first. Just before she lost sight of the BMW in her rearview mirror Vasia was sure she saw the BMW suddenly lurched forward at speed noticing how far the Astra now was.

Regardless of what speed she was doing and paying no heed to all the twists and turns, the BMW soon caught up.

"Shit, what am I going to do?" Vasia asked herself, getting increasingly upset and desperate.

"I would take the next right." A voice from the passenger seat said.

"What the fuck?" Vasia screamed.

She almost lost control of the car as it veered into the oncoming lane, but she quickly managed to regain control again and moved back into her lane at the last minute before a Land Rover went past angrily beeping and flashing his lights at her.

She looked over at the passenger seat and saw an attractive black lady in tribal clothing and braids in her hair sitting there. She was focused on the right turn that was coming up and was disappointed that they drove straight past it.

"You missed it."

"What?"

"You missed the turning."

It took Vasia a moment to figure out why this lady looked so familiar, and then she remembered where she saw her last.

"Ermee?"

"Hello," Ermee answered with her dazzling white smile.

"What? How?" Was all Vasia could manage as she continued to drive her Astra at speed along the country roads.

"We need to talk." Ermee declared

"Hell yeah, we need to talk." Vasia countered. "Why are you in my car? How the hell did you get in here?" And then, "You know, my husband is flying halfway across the world to find you?"

Ermee counted the answers to Vasia's questions on her hand. "I've come to help you. I teleported. I know, and everything will be ok with him."

"What do I need help with?"

Ermee answered by turning to look out the back window at the BMW that was still following them.

Knowing she had made an excellent point, one of her other answers suddenly clicked in Vasia's head. "Hang on. What do you mean, teleported?"

"I'm sure you must realise by now that your husband is coming to terms with newly acquired, shall we say, a special set of powers."

"He's working through some stuff. I don't know if we should call…"

"And." Ermee interrupted, "You must have wondered how he acquired these powers."
Vasia paused for a moment. The question had crossed her mind, but she was afraid of what the answer might be.

"I wouldn't worry, Vasia. Your husband has gone on a journey to find some answers. Once he has found these answers, he will emerge a changed man. A better man."

Vasia's insecurities started to show when she asked. "If he's a changed man. What does that mean for us?"

"It need not mean anything. Or it could mean everything. It all depends on what you want it to mean." Ermee answered cryptically.

Before Vasia could ask what the hell that meant, Ermee carried on "But we can see that you are a special woman and we can see something special happening to the both of you in the future. The time will come when you will need to step up, and I'm sure you will."

Several moments passed as Vasia tried to process what Ermee was saying. She was still concentrating on trying to drive as well with the BMW behind them.

"Simon said that's what your grandfather said to him just before…" Vasia let the sentence trail off, thinking of all the implications. Another thought came to her. "Hang on, are you saying that I will get powers as well?"

"As I have said before, you and he can mean everything or nothing. It all depends on you. Now, I recommend you turn right here."

Vasia did as Ermee recommended. After a few more right and left turns, they eventually found themselves driving into the bustling, concrete jungle, centre of Hemel Hempstead. Vasia could see the BMW was still easily following them.

"Now. Do you think we should lose these people?" Ermee asked.

She was leaning forward in her seat and had both her hands on the dashboard.

"I don't think we can. My Astra cannot outrun that BMW."

"I said nothing about outrunning them," Ermee said with a mysterious smile.

Vasia briefly saw that her hands were glowing orange.

"Turn left here. Ermee urgently commanded.

"But it's one way."

"Quick, do it."

In a panic, Vasia immediately turned the wheel hard left before they missed the turning. The wheels squealed in protest. She could hear a few passer-bys cursing her on noticing this minor infringement and she had the presence of mind to feel momentarily embarrassed.

They were out of sight of the BMW for just a few seconds.

"Brake." Ermee commanded again, her glowing hands increased in intensity.

On instinct, Vasia performed an emergency stop expecting to hit something.

The back streets of Hemel Hempstead disappeared, and they were somewhere else.

It took Vasia a few moments to realise where. "How the hell are we back at my house?" She positively shouted in disbelief.

"I told you I can teleport," Ermee said casually as if that explained everything. "And I can teleport things around me if I'm touching it."

"What???" Vasia asked, almost hyperventilating.

"I said I…"

"I know what you just said." Vasia interrupted, almost shouting. Then calming down a bit. "Is that what Simon can do?" Not bothering to wait for Ermee to reply, she added. "Why the fuck did he catch a plane for?"

Ignoring her curses and presumably taking her shouting for what it was, shock, Ermee replied somewhat cryptically, "No, it's only women who have the power to teleport." Then she added, "But when your husband realises his full potential, he will be able to do much, much more."

Ermee let it sink in for a bit before she said. "Well, that's me done. I've got to go. Remember what I said. This could all mean nothing, or it could mean everything. You decide." And with that, she disappeared with an undramatic pop.

For several moments Vasia sat in the car trying to calm down and gather her thoughts.

*

The Astra led Stone and Haider right into the middle of Hemel Hempstead, and when they thought she would get caught in traffic, they observed Mrs. Emerson taking an immediate hard left into a one-way road, causing her wheels to squeal in protest.

"What is she playing at?" Haider was confused.

All Stone could do was shrug his shoulders.

Moments later, when they rounded the corner, they both looked confused.

150

Haider was the first to ask. "Ok, where did she go?"

For several moments they sat there dumbfounded. Until a car came up the right way up the one-way street. The occupant angrily beeped his horn and gave the two detectives the finger.

Stone waved at the guy apologetically. He manoeuvred to the side and climbed up to the curb to let the guy get past.

Haider noticed instead of thanking them, the occupant of the other car cursed them some more as he passed and drove off.

Shaking his head at the rudeness of some people, Haider turned to Stone and asked, "Was that someone else in the car with her?"

"I'm not sure. How can someone get in the car while it was moving? Unless she was hiding beforehand."

After a few moments, Haider asked, "Shall we go to their house and talk to her?"

Before he even finished uttering the question, his mobile phone pinged. He took it out of his suit breast pocket and noted who the text was from.

"It's from Terry. He's got something else for us back at the Yard." he explained.

"Mrs. Emerson will have to wait. Let's see what Terry has for us first and then we can go visit the lady later."

Haider nodded in agreement. After carefully reversing back out of the one-way road, they made their way back to London and to Scotland Yard.

Chapter 20

Your flight eventually touched down in Cairo at 3 AM local time. The sun was not even up yet, but it was still extremely hot and humid. The heat hit you like a slap to the face as soon as you had disembarked from the plane.

The interior of Cairo International Airport was clean, well ventilated and spacious, with marble flooring covering the entire area and potted palm trees dotting all over the place.

You noticed a massive security presence. You chalked this down as the reason for the lengthy delay of getting through passport control.

Eventually, an hour later, you were through security control but was still in the middle of the airport.

You discovered, in your haste to get on the next plane here, that it hadn't crossed your mind during the nineteen-hour stopover in Cairo if you wanted to use the time to go sightseeing, you would actually need a visa to step out of the airport.

Therefore, with one hour already down, you were stuck in this airport for the rest of it too.

Watching people enter and exit the airport you were stuck for something to do. That was until of all places to see one you noticed an Irish pub near the duty-free shop.

The big green neon sign on the front designated the pub *"Harry's"*. There was a four-leaf clover in place of the 'a'.

Feeling a little lost and overwhelmed for being in a foreign country that you had not been too and seeing the familiar caused you to make a beeline straight for it.

Moments later, you were propped up at the bar. Considering the early hour, the pub was quiet and practically empty save for one of two business types in suits tapping away on their keyboards.

There was one solitary member of staff at the bar, a tall, friendly-looking, bald, Egyptian man. He looked friendly enough, with a smile on his face but his physique was quite intimidating. He reminded you of a wrestler with his white shirt barely containing his bulging muscles.

You got talking to him and found out he had the intriguing name of Kosey.

"So, where are you from?" Kosey asked you conversationally after he had handed you a bottle of Sakara Gold.

You quickly realised that despite being called an Irish pub, this place didn't actually serve any Irish or British beverages.

"I'm from Luton in England," you answered.

"As in the airport?" Kosey asked a trifle confused.

You couldn't help but chuckle; You were used to this question. Years ago, when you had been on holiday in Newquay and sitting in a cafe overlooking Fistral Beach, you had had a similar conversation with the cafe owner who thought Luton was just an airport in London. It blew his mind when he realised people actually lived there. It seems either Luton has a bad rep for being the second ugliest town in the UK or not a town at all. The place can't win.

"No, the town. The airport is on the outskirts of it," you answered.

You and Kosey carried on talking for another twenty minutes or so until, suddenly looking over your shoulder, Kosey asked rather ominously, "Did you come by yourself, Simon?"

"Yes, why?" you asked. A feeling of dread grew inside you.

"I think someone's following you. Don't look, but a man in a suit came in just after you did. He is sitting down at a booth behind you pretending to read a paper but has been staring at you with unusual interest. He hasn't even ordered a drink." Kosey said. The last sentence had a hint of reproach as if someone had the nerve to sit in his establishment for this long and not order a drink.

Not able to help yourself and despite being warned not to, you swivelled around on your barstool and looked toward the suited man in the booth.

You found his shaved head, square jaw and piercing eyes intimidating. Deep down you had a bad spine tingling feeling about this guy.

The first thing that you could think to say was, "Do you think we should ask him if he wants a drink?" and you gave a nervous chuckle at your own spontaneous lousy joke.

The man in the booth, realising he had been made, suddenly stood up and walked out of the pub. But not before giving a meaningful look in your direction.

"Do you know him?" Kosey asked.

You turned back around, confused. "No, but he looks familiar, I think he was on the same flight that I was on." Then after a moment's thought with misplaced hopefulness, you added, "Maybe he's waiting for a connecting flight like I am."

"Hmmm, a bit coincidental, I think," Kosey answered cynically. "Besides, I have seen his type before, government types, they're bad news."

"Government types?" you echoed, sitting straight to attention. "As in special agent, that type of government type?"

Kosey nodded solemnly.

"Boy!" you said, taking a final swig of your beer. "The first time I've travelled this far to an exotic country, and a secret agent is following me."

"Must make you feel like *James Bond*," Kosey acknowledged. "Do you know why he's following you?"

You didn't know, but considering what had happened to you in the past week, paranoia started seeping in.

Kosey, as if noticing the growing look of apprehension on your face, added, "You don't look like the kind of guy who a secret agent would be following." And then maybe thinking your look of apprehension may be part of something more profound, he added conspiratorially, "But I always say never judge a book by its cover."

Instantly noticing the change in Kosey's tone, you looked at him and said, "That might be a story I'll tell you later." And then, turning back to the door, you added, "I am going to find out why that guy is following me."

You stood up from your barstool, and with a sense of purpose, you left the pub. You could feel Kosey staring at your fast retreating back.

As soon as you stepped out of the Irish pub, you started looking for your stalker. You didn't have to look for long. About 100 yards away, leaning on a palm tree by some bins. He was trying to look nonchalant but failing.

Your stalker didn't notice you walking towards him at first. But as you got closer, he spotted you. He immediately turned 180 and power walked in the opposite direction.

"Hey," you shouted, but the stalker just started walking faster.

This caused you to increase speed too. You even broke into a quick run when the stalker went past a currency exchange kiosk and momentarily lost from sight.

After passing the kiosk, you immediately caught sight of him again and allowed yourself to slow down to a fast walk.

"Hey. You. stop!" you shouted again.

But instead of stopping, the stalker broke into a run. You immediately gave chase.

The stalker was obviously fit and healthy and had lots of stamina to run the speed he was going. But you could run faster. Therefore, within moments, you had almost caught up to him.

The stalker, somehow sensing that you were directly behind him, took you by surprise when he suddenly stopped, turned on his heel, took you by the scruff of your shirt and, using your own momentum, picked you up and threw you down onto your back on the marble floor.

It happened so fast that you had no chance to register what was going on. Momentarily winded, you could see stars—the result of whacking your head on the floor.

The back of your head felt warm and wet. When you put your hand back there your fingers came back bloody. Yet, when you put your hand to your head a second time, you couldn't feel the wound. It had already healed.

Despite the situation, you had the presence of mind to be slightly taken aback. You were not yet used to your super quick healing. A passer-by offering to help you stand up broke you out of your reverie.

You gladly accepted the help. Once up, you quickly brushed yourself off, and after spotting the stalker again on the far end of the Food Court, you gave chase again.

The stalker must have heard you running behind him because he looked around. You could see the look of surprise on the man's face before he turned tail and ran.

The two of you sprinted through the busy Food Court, with the stalker rudely shoving people out of the way.

You were gaining on the stalker when you witnessed him bumping into an elderly Indian lady in a hijab. The lady would fall to the floor with a nasty bump if you hadn't got to her in time and caught her just before her head hit the floor.

"Are you ok?" you asked the lady as you helped her regain her balance.

The old lady smiled appreciatively, but when she spoke, it was in a foreign language.

Having learned a thing or two from living with Vasia for so long, you recognised it as Farsi and knew she had said, "Thank-you."

"You're welcome," you automatically replied in Farsi with a smile.

You left the old lady in search of your stalker.

You exited the busy Food Court and stopped for a moment.

You couldn't see any sign of the man. He wasn't straight in front of you where the entrance to the walkway to all the departure gates was.

You looked to your left. Escalators were going up to a mezzanine with shops. There was no sign of the man up there.

He couldn't have made it up the escalator already! Could he?

You heard a noise and looked to your right, just in time to see the door to the men's restroom close. You hadn't seen the stalker go in, but it was only reasonable to assume that he did, given the time you had lost sight of him and the fact that this area was quiet with very few people around.

Carefully you opened the door and entered the men's restroom. You found yourself in a cream porcelain-tiled corridor that was about twenty feet long before it led to the restroom proper.

Being as quiet and stealthy as possible, you tried not to breathe too heavily as you slowly walked down the corridor.

You were getting to the end of it when a strange feeling came over you. It was like the feeling you had when you were in *The Kings Arms* toilets the other day and then the motorway accident yesterday. You were having a vision.

In the vision, you were walking to the end of the corridor. Like you were doing so now when The Stalker stepped out from a corner. He was mere inches away and bashed you over the head with something substantial and metal.

You snapped out of your vision.

Without thinking you put your arm out to the right.

You caught the man's arm, stopping him from bashing you over the head with some metal object.

"Whoa," With a look of stupid surprise, you turned to the man.

The guy also had a dumb look of surprise on his face as he stared slack-jawed at you. Must have been wondering how you blocked him without looking.

The look of surprise turned to a snarl as the stalker shook off your grip and stepping back a pace he pointed the metal object at your head.

With no experience with this apart from what you see in movies and video games, as a layman, you simply recognised the object as a gun. A professional would know that it was a Walther P99 semi-automatic pistol.

"Whoa," you said again, this time putting both your arms up in the air, suddenly alarmed.

The thought of chasing this stranger across the airport may not have been your brightest idea ran fleetingly across your mind.

"N-n-no need to get violent." you stammered fearfully, "I just want to know who you are."

"Need to know, berk," the stalker growled shortly.

With the accent and insult, you could tell he was Cockney.

"Why were you following me?"

The stalker just shrugged, as if to emphasise the same answer.

"Who do you think I am?"

You didn't get to finish your question when the entrance to the restroom opened, and in walked a middle-aged African man in a business suit.

On instinct, the stalker turned to the man, levelling his gun on him.

The man stopped dead in his tracks, took one look at the situation, and decided he wasn't that desperate to go to the toilet. Calmly, he immediately reversed out of the restroom.

Taking advantage of the distraction, you rushed the stalker to wrestle the gun out of his hand.

The stalker, however, had extremely quick reflexes and was ready for this. He stepped to the side, and with his free arm, using your momentum once more, he pushed you headfirst into one of the porcelain sinks. The sink broke under your weight, and you fell to the ground.

Momentarily stunned, you rolled over onto your back to see the stalker standing over, pointing the gun at you. Realising too late what would happen next, your eyes widened in fear.

Showing no emotion, the man leveled the gun at your chest and fired.

For you the world went black.

The stalker calmly spent some time wiping his gun with a rag from his pocket and then holstered it.

"God damnit." he cursed when he spotted some of your blood had splattered on his shirt. He cursed again when he looked in the mirror and discovered some of it was on his face too.

He took a few moments to splash some water over his face. When he was satisfied that he was clean he straightened up, took one casual look at your body on the floor and calmly sashayed out of the restroom whistling, as he would say, his favourite stewed prune.

You laid motionless on the floor for God knows how long. Eyes closed, not breathing, with a gaping hole in your chest and blood pooling around you.

Eventually the wound started healing, and as it closed, you took a deep breath, your eyes flashed open, and you sat bolt upright.

"Motherfucker!" was the first thing you screamed, to the now empty bathroom. Dying really hurts. You put your hand to your chest where the wound should be, but it was gone.

Shakily you stood up using one of the sinks that you hadn't broken before as support. You took a moment to look in all the stalls to confirm that you were on your own now. The bathroom was empty.

Wondering where your murderer had got to, you looked at yourself in the mirror. You appeared to be alive, but you were a mess. Apart from the bloody hole in your t-shirt, practically the whole of your back was covered in your own blood when it had pooled around your body, you couldn't tell someone had shot you!

Wearily you uttered an expletive again. You would need a change of clothes, but your clothes were all in your backpack. Your backpack was currently in hold.

For what seemed like forever, you just stood staring at yourself in the mirror. You were visibly shaken out of the shock of being shot and dying. Also, you were feeling self-conscious. You would have to go out in public looking like that.

Eventually, you mentally pulled yourself together and took a deep breath. Trying to look calm and collected, as if you were meant to be there, you casually exited the restroom. You took a moment to look this way and that to make sure the guy that had shot you was not about. Then you aimed for the Irish pub with your hands in your pockets.

*

Unfortunately, if you had looked up when you came out of the restroom you would have seen who you were looking for. Up on the mezzanine leaning against the metal and glass frame wall overlooking the food court and toilets below was your stalker conversing with someone on his mobile phone.

The person he needed to speak to was on fast dial, and on the second ring, they picked up.

"Yes, the target has been eliminated," The stalker said in answer to the person's first question.

"What? You killed him?" The voice angrily asked.

"It couldn't have been avoided. He made me and went after me. It was self-defence."

"Very well. If it couldn't be helped, make sure you come back quickly for the next phase."

"Yes, I will get the next flight back immediately."

"Make sure you do." The person on the other end said and then without so much as a goodbye; there was an audible click as they hung up.

The stalker sighed and quietly swore under his breath as pocketed his mobile. "What a right merchant."

He had never met the face behind the voice before. Didn't even know his actual name. Just his code name Mr. D. But he could tell he was a bit of a dick.

He was about to walk away and find out when the next flight back home was when something out of the corner of his eye caused him to stop and do a double-take.

"Bloody hell?" he said under his breath.

He stared down at the floor below watching you, apparently alive and kicking, walk out of the toilets and started heading back to the pub.

It took him a while to Adam and Eve what his eyes were seeing. Eventually, he headed down the escalator and followed you.

Chapter 21

You were anxious and a little paranoid as you wondered if anyone would notice and stop you, over your bloody appearance. A few people threw a cursory glance your way but did not show any particular interest in your appearance.

There was a scary moment when you noticed two, armed Airport security guards standing in your way.

They seemed to be engrossed in a conversation with some other security guard over a walkie-talkie. They had their backs to you at first. As you got closer to them, the guard on the other end of the walkie-talkie seemingly gave them a command. With a sense of purpose, they turned in the direction that you were coming from, just as you walked past them. They walked off.

You gave an enormous sigh of relief. You couldn't believe your luck that they hadn't seen you, despite just being inches away from them.

Five minutes later, you reached the Irish pub without further incident. Inside you went straight up to the bar where Kosey was in the middle of wiping a glass dry with a clean rag.

It took him a few moments to look up from his task and realise that you were standing opposite him from across the bar. The first thing he noticed was the state of your clothes.

"Whoa, what the hell happened to you? Has someone died?"

"Yes," you answered. "I did." And then when Kosey gave a look that you took to mean confusion, you added, "I will tell you everything, but I need your help." Then after looking down at yourself. "And a change of clothes."

"Of course." Kosey opened the bar hatch door and motioned for you to follow him.

You walked behind the bar and followed Kosey down a little corridor behind it and into an office.

Sparsely decorated, the office was dimly lit by a single naked bulb. There was a green two-seater sofa on one end of the room with an old, battered-looking filing cabinet beside it.

On the other end of the room, there was a desk with two bar stools serving as office chairs. On top of the desk was a messy collection of ad hoc paperwork that consisted of a mix of invoices and receipts. Also, on the desk against the wall were four small wide-screen colour TV monitors. On three of the monitors, you recognised the pub from different viewpoints. One viewpoint was at the bar looking towards the entrance. The second was the opposite of the entranceway looking towards the bar. The third was a bird's-eye view of the actual bar itself. But it was the fourth TV that caught your attention the most. It took you a few moments to realise what it was showing, but the dark red pool on the floor made it a dead giveaway that this was the restroom you had just come from.

Your eyes widened, and you whirled round to face Kosey, who had been silently standing behind you.

You were about to ask what the hell was going on when you noticed that Kosey's usual jolly demeanour had disappeared into a solemn, determined look. Also, he was holding a knife.

"You need not explain what's going on," Kosey said, raising the knife with his right hand.

"Now hang on a minute," you said immediately panicking, but you didn't get to finish your sentence.

Kosey suddenly brought the knife down and stabbed himself in his left hand.

Kosey then pulled said knife out and held his hand out for you to see.

You didn't know whether you should have been feeling horrified, panicked, confused, or disgusted. Or all of the above.

"Because," Kosey continued, as his hand healed, "You and I are the same."

"How?" was all you could think to ask.

Kosey looked at the bank of security monitors and noticed a customer was at the bar.

"Wait here for a minute while I serve this customer, and then I will tell you everything."

Kosey left the office to serve the said customer, leaving you standing alone in the office, digesting what had just happened.

"Holy shit." You said to yourself on a few occasions.

Less than three minutes later, Kosey came back with a neatly folded pair of jeans and a white t-shirt that had the quote "I Love Cairo" on the front with a red heart replacing the word "Love". He also had two bottles of Sakara Gold. He offered one bottle to you and gave you the clothes to change into. Once you had changed and, feeling ridiculous in the t-shirt, the two of you talked.

*

You were still chatting two hours later.

Occasionally interrupted by the odd customer or two coming to the bar, you spoke about your powers, how you both got them and who else had them. It turned out that you both knew Eraaf and Ermee.

"How did we get these powers?" You asked at one point.

"I'm not one hundred percent sure, but I think the Xuholos are a race of mystical super-beings, and Eraaf is the strongest of them. They go around the world and 'give' powers to people that they think worthy." Kosey used his fingers as quotations when he said the word "give".

"So, there are more people like us?"

"Yes, there are more than a dozen I know about."

"Why has nobody heard about these Xuholo people before or about the people they have given superpowers before?"

"They are very secretive. When you find them, they will persuade you to keep in the shadows, be secretive like them, only use your powers for good and only when it doesn't put your identity and their identity at risk."

"What happens if I do put their identity at risk?" you asked, thinking of the day on the motorway.

"Then, they will take your powers back?" Kosey answered matter-of-factly.

"What powers have we got?" you queried.

"We're all different. Some have more powers than most. For instance, I seem to only be able to heal quickly, and I have super strength," Kosey said. "You, however, seem to be the full package."

"What do you mean?"

"Well, there are your visions, you can heal, and you're immortal like me."

"Immortal?" you echoed incredulously. "As in I don't age?"

Kosey nodded, and then after you pondered for a few moments.

"How old are you?"

"I am over 120 years old." And then when I could only stare slack-jawed at him, Kosey added, chuckling, "I know, I don't look a day over twenty-five. Which incidentally is the age I got my powers."

"What happened to you to get your powers?"

"To cut a long story short, I was a soldier in the Egyptian army during World War Two. My regiment fought alongside the British and Australians against the Axis powers."

"I was there during the Battles of Alamein and Alam el Halfa in 1942, fighting the German Afrika Korps. One day I got badly injured trying to save a civilian from being shot. It turns out that civilian was one of the Xuholos and while I was lying in a hospital bed, seconds from dying, he came to my side, healed me with his hands and gave me my powers.

After that, I helped the Allied forces in Libya and Tunisia. Believe me, my super healing and super strength was a significant help, especially during the Battle of Kasserine Pass in 43 when I got split from my regiment and got ambushed by a group of tanks of the Afrika Korps. I single-handedly destroyed them all."

You could tell Kosey was rather proud of this last statement.

"Did anyone find out about your superpowers?"

"Until then, no. Maybe some Afrika Korps saw, but I killed them all, so they don't count. It wasn't until two months later; I was at Djebel Tahent. The Americans were there at the time and helped in the Battle of Hill 609.

The American General, Bradley I think his name was, saw my potential when he somehow caught sight of me displaying my powers. To this day, I don't know how, but he gave me an assignment that is, shall we say, a story for another day." Kosey said this last bit while conspiratorially tapping his nose.

Knowing when not to press further, you asked: "Was it Eraaf who healed you?"

"Yes, and don't ask me how old he is, I've given up guessing. He looked the same age then as he does now. Also, piecing together what others have told me during the years I believed he might be several centuries old. Maybe even a millennia or two."

Trying to process all this information was daunting.

Finally you asked: "So, different people can have different powers?"

"Yeah everybody's default power is immortality but women seem to have the added advantage of being able to teleport. And, from the people I know of, there is a lady in America who can fly and has bulletproof skin. There is a guy in France who can breathe underwater, another in Ukraine who can shape-shift. Apart from you, there are two other people in the UK. One is an autistic kid. By kid, I mean he was a kid when he gained his superpowers, and as he's immortal, it's anyone's guess what his actual age is. And by autistic I mean that's the best way normal society can describe him. He is sensitive to light and sound and is non-verbal. In reality, he can see and hear more than we can and can actually talk to machines. I hear he makes a living by constantly moving from place to place and links to an ATM to get money whenever he wants. The second person is a mystery even to us mysterious group of people. It seems his only power is immortality. But he is a kick-ass son of a bitch who over the centuries, has amassed lots of skills in various forms of martial arts, mostly in sword fighting."

You thought for a moment, and then inspiration struck and asked, "Do you ever team up to save the world?"

"No, we're not *The Avengers*, you know," Kosey said with hints of contempt and boredom as if he had been asked this question before, "Besides as I have said before, the Xuholos prefers us to stay in the shadows, it's almost a condition for us to have our superpowers, we don't wear any tight-fitting superhero costumes or have any cheesy superhero names. I'm just Kosey, and you're just Simon."

You felt almost disappointed.

"You said I'm the full package. How do you know?"

"Well, you said you can run really fast?"

"Yeah but not as fast as the Flash or anything."

"I reckon if you practise, hone your skills; you potentially could run as fast as a speeding bullet, maybe faster," Kosey said then added, "Also over the one hundred years I seem to have developed a nose for these things, I can tell when looking at people what powers they have. It's kinda like another superpower of mine. And I can see so much potential in you to develop more superpowers, including super strength like me. You might be the most powerful person in the world and not know about it."

At that point, Kosey had to go out to the bar to serve another customer. You were left alone again to contemplate what he had said.

A few minutes later, Kosey came back, and he continued, "I've met the guy in the UK, the kick-ass one, by the name of Arthur. He came over here for a few years and taught me how to fight. I recommend you look him up when you get back and ask him to teach you, especially if you will have secret agents following you around. Like now."

"What do you mean?" you asked, suddenly alert.

"It looks like that secret agent friend of yours is hovering around. I clocked him when I was out just now serving a customer. You can just about see him on the security monitors."

You immediately swivelled around on the bar stool that you had been sitting on and looked at the security monitors for your stalker, secret agent friend.

It took a few moments, but you could just make out the guy on the monitor that was overlooking the entrance. He was standing guard outside the pub, keeping a watchful eye on everyone that walked past, as if he was waiting for someone. You didn't have to be told who that someone was.

Still staring at the screen, you said to Kosey, "You said this guy I need to find in the UK taught you how to fight?"

"Yes."

"Do you think you can teach me some moves?"

"How long till your flight?"

You looked at your watch. "About fourteen hours before they start boarding,"

"I can teach you a little, but we really need more than fourteen hours." And then looking thoughtfully at the security monitor, Kosey added, "What do you think to some 'on the job' training?"

Looking serious, you turned to Kosey, "Sounds great." Then inspiration struck, and you couldn't help but smile. "Sounds like we're going to team up. Like *The Avengers*."

Kosey shook his head and rolled his eyes.

Chapter 22

Kosey gave you a quick crash course in how to wrestle a gun from someone. Ten minutes later the two of you exited the pub and went straight up to the Stalker.

The Stalker was leaning absentmindedly against a palm tree with his arms crossed, occasionally looking to his left and right as people passed him. For a moment, he didn't notice Kosey and you standing in front of him. When he did, he suddenly rose to attention. His hand instinctively went for his gun holstered on his belt.

Kosey wagged his finger "Not here," he said authoritatively, "Let's take this someplace else."

He nodded to the security guards not far off from where they were standing to indicate this was not an appropriate place to do whatever they wanted to do.
The stalker nodded in agreement and quietly, in single file, the three of you walked back into the pub.

After nodding to the attractive olive-skinned woman who had started her shift to replace Kosey, he directed you behind the bar and down the corridor at the back. Instead of going into the office, you went down some steep stone steps that led to a big concrete, air-conditioned, open-plan room.

The many barrels of beer and various crates of bottles of wine and champagne and more made it apparent this was the beer cellar. You could not hear the noise from the bar meaning the room was soundproofed.

As you got to the middle of the room, you and Kosey turned to face the Stalker, who immediately unholstered his gun and pointed it at both of you.

"What's your name, friend?" Kosey sounded relaxed and casual enough, but his emphasis on the word friend implied that he knew this man was anything but.

"None of your business?" the stalker said shortly, then he turned to you, "I shot you. You should be bloody brown bread," he added matter-of-factly.

"What's bread got to do with it," Kosey asked, confused by the Stalker's cockney.

"You must have missed," you replied smartly, straight-faced.

"No, I didn't, I never miss. I saw the bullet go into your chest."

"Then you must be seeing things."

"Don't get all lemon tart with me," the Stalker said, steadily getting angrier and angrier. He came a couple of steps closer to you with his gun, still pointing at your head. "Tell me who you are and why you are not dead?"

"Remember what I taught you, Simon?" Kosey suddenly said.

You nodded, with a steely look in your eyes and a misplaced sense of bravado, you grabbed the man's wrist with the gun. Before he could react, you pointed it away, spun around so that you had your back to the stalker, twisted his arm, and, using all your strength, you flipped the guy over and onto the ground.

With your free hand, you wrestled the gun out of the Stalker's hand by twisting it to the right and breaking the stalker's trigger finger in the process. Even though the room was soundproofed you wondered if his scream was heard upstairs.

Now, you ask yourself how much more effective that would have been if you were a professional fighter and hadn't had only ten minutes of training on how to do this.

What in fact happened was this: You grabbed the stalker's wrist, and accidentally nudged the guy's trigger finger. This resulted in getting shot point-blank in the head. With a bloody hole the size of a fifty pence piece in your head, you crumpled unceremoniously to the floor, dead.

Kosey face palmed himself, "If you need a job doing.." He started. He turned to the stalker who was in the process of levelling the gun on him. He promptly punched him in the face and he dropped to the floor out cold. "…do it yourself." Kosey finished

*

Several moments later, you sat bolt upright, swearing as you did before in the airport restroom.

The first thing you noticed was Kosey tying the Stalker to a simple wooden chair with rope.

Judging by the red swelling on the Stalker's head you guessed that Kosey had stepped in after you had died to finish your job.

As you stood up brushing yourself off, you saw some of your brain matter covering the wall nearby and grimaced.

Hearing you stand up, Kosey turned around and appeared unsurprised that you were alive. He handed you some of the Stalker's possessions and said, "Here, make yourself useful and go through these."

Feeling slightly embarrassed, you did as he asked.

*

The Stalker woke up dazed. When he was able to get his eyes to focus, he stared unflummoxed. You couldn't tell if his look was a question or confusion. You and Kosey stood in front of him.

"I shot you in the head," the Stalker growled, "You should be dead. Again!"

"You missed. Again!" was your reply.

"Who the hell are you?" Although the man was angry, there was a hint of awe in that question.

"The question is, who are you?" Kosey asked.

"Need to know," the man growled again.

"Well, fortunately for us, while you were asleep, we went through your pockets and found your wallet," you said, waving it in the air.

"Don't you dare touch that, that is private property,"

"Oops," you said as you flipped open the wallet, "We kinda already touched it."

You took out a white plastic card with a photo of the man's face and his current employment details.

"And we have found out you are Sean Orenglas, Counter-Terrorism Officer at Scotland Yard." You paused, "Now, what is a Counter-Terrorism Officer from Scotland Yard doing following me?"

"Countering terrorism," Sean replied smartly.

"But I'm not a terrorist," you responded defensively.

"That's what all the terrorists say."

You changed the subject. "I know two other people from Scotland Yard. Detective Stone and Special Agent Haider. They came to my house the other day to ask me questions about anything I may have witnessed at the Green Park Tube Station terrorist attack in London last week. Did they send you after me?"

"I can't say. Need to know."

You took that as a yes. "Why?"

Sean looked like he was about to say, "Need to know," again, when he thought better of it.

"Look, I really can't say. They just said I needed to follow you as you were a person of interest. You were not meant to see me."

"That went well for you, didn't it," Kosey said sarcastically and then to you he said, "Come on, if you still want to learn to fight before you catch your flight, I'll take you to the gym?"

"Ohh the airport has a gym," you said, impressed, as the two of you made for the door to the cellar.

"Hey?" Sean shouted to your retreating backs, "What about me?"

"You can stay there and think about what you have just done," Kosey answered mockingly.

"Don't want you following me when I catch my flight," you added.

"Where are you catching your flight to?" Sean asked, hopefully, as if you would really tell him.

You paused in the doorway, looking thoughtful. You turned back to Sean, and before disappearing from view and closing the door, you muttered, "To answer your first question. Find out who I am."

*

Minutes later, you and Kosey were standing in what served as the airport gym. It was in the basement, so it was windowless but was well lit by LED strip lights embedded in the ceiling all the way along the one-hundred-foot space. Large air-conditioning units were hanging from the ceiling, making the room feel very cool.

The upbeat, high tempo music played a little too loudly from the speaker system.

The gym, well equipped with one half of it containing rows of fancy-looking treadmills, cross-country ski machines, elliptical trainers, stair steppers, and at least another half dozen other types of cardio equipment all pointing in one direction looking at a bank of wide-screen televisions on the wall. In the other half of the gym were all the strength equipment, including dip stations, various types of bench presses, calf machines, and leg press machines. There was an area with racks of dumbbells of different weights and a row of exercise mats.

At the moment you and Kosey were the only two people so you could comfortably do what needed to be done without questions asked.

Standing on the exercise mats facing each other, you had both changed into gym gear with Kosey wearing a sleeveless black top, which seemed to amplify his already muscular physique, and you were wearing a red sleeveless top. Although you had been developing a bit of a six-pack since the accident, compared to Kosey, you looked like a skinny little runt and felt conscious about it.

"Right," Kosey was saying, "I know various forms of martial arts, including a few styles of wrestling; Freestyle, Bokh and Luta Livre. I also know Judo, Hapkido, and Krav Maga."

"Impressive," you answered smartly.

"It is. We only have thirteen hours, so I'm just going to teach you the basics from each of them. Let's start with some wrestling. The first thing you need to know is how to shoot."

"Shoot?" you asked incredulously, "I didn't realise wrestling had guns?" you added smartly.

Feeling awkward apparently brought out the comedian in you.

Kosey shook his head. "No, 'shoot' is a basic wrestling move that you perform as a foundation for most takedowns. I'll show you. You start off in a staggered stance, lowering your body towards the ground, so you're lower than your opponent, like this."

Kosey lowered his body bending his back slightly.

"Then, you step forward and drop to your knee with your dominant leg." Kosey moved forward towards you and dropped to his knee.

"Kosey, we've only known each other for a few hours, I don't think this is the right time to propose!"

Ignoring your smart-alec comment, he said, "Carrying on with the momentum, with your other foot, you step closer until your knee is between your opponent's legs."

"Personal space, man!" you teased.

175

"And then from this, you can perform other moves like the double leg takedown."

"What's the doub…"

In one fluid movement, Kosey grabbed the backs of your calves, pulled them towards him, and went to stand up, lifting you up in the process and threw you back down on the mat.

From your perspective, one second you were standing, the next you were lying flat on your back, momentarily winded.

Kosey, towered above you and looked down. Grinning, he said, "That's the double leg takedown."

You stood up, all serious now because Kosey had wounded your pride.

You said, "Ok, teach me."

Kosey went through the process two more times and then said to you, "Ok, you try to do it to me now."

"But I won't be able to lift you. You look heavier than me."

"Weight doesn't matter. For one, you don't have to lift, if you use your momentum properly, you can just push, and I will fall. Besides, as I have said before, I think you may be a lot stronger than you think you are. Try it."

"Ok."

It was awkward and clumsy, but you tried it. You performed the first part of the shoot easily enough, but when you grabbed the backs of Kosey's legs, he didn't budge. You got a face full of unmovable muscle for your trouble too.

Kosey smiled again, "Try again, but faster. And don't stop. Remember, just follow through in one fluid movement."

You went into a staggered stance again. A look of determination spread across your face as you took in a deep breath.

"Remember," Kosey said, "you're a lot stronger than you think you are."

You took another deep breath. You felt a sense of primordial power coming up from your legs and flowed through your body.

You took a third deep breath.

What happened next happened quickly, but you felt like you were moving in slow motion. In one fluid movement, you dropped to your dominant knee. Then with your other foot, you stepped closer until one was behind Kosey's legs.

You grabbed the backs of his legs and lifted him up in the air. You lifted him with so much force that he somersaulted in midair and landed flat on his face on the mat.

Kosey looked up from eating a face full of mat at your astonished face. Although slightly winded, he laughed. "Ha, now we're talking!"

Kosey stood up and immediately faced you.

"How did I do that?" you asked bewildered.

"For just a split second, you believed and you tapped into your powers," Kosey explained. "Now, I want you to push me," he added.

"What?" you asked, confused.

"I want you to push me." As if to emphasise what he wanted, Kosey roughly shoved you in the chest—trying to get some sort of reaction.

"Oww. What are you doing?" you stuttered with a growing feeling of further confusion and fear.

"Push me," Kosey repeated, shoving you again.

It wasn't just confusion and fear. You felt anger starting to boil up inside. No, not anger. It was the feeling you had before. The one you can only describe as primordial power started rising inside again.

"Stop it," you snarled.

"Push me," Kosey repeated, almost shouting, shoving you even more.

The feeling of power felt like it was taking over your body. You could feel it rising all the way to your head.

Kosey went to shove you again.

"STOP!" You roared with a wrath that you hadn't felt before.

With all your might you shoved Kosey in the chest. All 131 kilograms of him went flying like a rocket down the entire length of the gym. He collided with the row of treadmills, sending them flying like skittles.

You watched him fly. You were sure his expression turned from surprise to a smile with a cheeky wink before he collided with the treadmills.

"Holy shit," you said to yourself, looking at your hands.

As Kosey untangled himself from the mass of treadmills and started walking back up the entire length of the gym, you felt slightly anxious that he and his big hulk of a body might retaliate.

"I'm so sorry," you said.

"Don't be," Kosey reassured and then more serious, "Now, I can really start training you."

As he got closer, he launched into a sprint and letting out a scream he leaped into the air. Before you knew it, he delivered a well-placed kick to your head.

*

Hours later, your bodies were both covered with sweat, and your clothes were damp. Kosey was finally finishing his teaching with the basics of the roundhouse kick. You forget how many times you had tried it, but finally you went into the guard stance. Fists up, you moved forward on your left leg, brought your right leg up bent so that your knee was pointing out to the side. Then with a quick, crushing kick, you struck Kosey in the neck. With a grunt, he fell to the floor.

Usually, that would have knocked out an average person, but Kosey jumped up within seconds. He rubbed his neck and turned his head to the left and right, making it creak.

"Ok," Kosey said, slightly winded. "That was good. Remember, an important aspect of getting a good powerful kick is your breathing. If you can control your breathing, you're less likely to run out of steam, and it's possible to exert more force if you can synchronise your breathing with the kick. But I think that's all for now."

"So, you reckon I'm ready to fight then?"

"This isn't *The Matrix*. This is no 'I know Kung Fu' situation. You'll need months, maybe years of extensive training with our friend Arthur. But I reckon you will stand your ground in a normal street fight," Kosey admitted with a little caution.

"But now that I know I have super strength, I guess I'm kind of unbeatable," you said with a hint of ignorant pride.

"Fighting isn't always about strength," Kosey admonished. "What all the martial arts try to teach you is that you can use your opponent's strength against them. Remember, at the start, when I was showing you the double leg takedown. I said if you use your momentum correctly, strength doesn't come into it."

You said nothing to that as you quietly digested what Kosey had said to you.

"Ok, we better get changed, you don't want to miss your flight," Kosey added.

"And we should check our friend in your beer cellar," you added as the two of you walked to the doors leading out of the gym. "He's been down there for almost twelve hours; he must at least be desperate for a pee!"

*

After showering and changing, you were both standing in the doorway to the beer cellar. Apart from the bottles, cans, crates, and barrels of alcohol. There was a chair with freshly cut rope sitting on the seat.

"Shit, where did he go?" you asked dumbfounded.

All you and Kosey could do was stare at the empty chair.

Chapter 23

Moments later, the two of you were back in Kosey's office, looking over the security camera footage.

"Can't see any sign of him," Kosey was saying. "You will have to go and just watch your back."

"Maybe he's given up and gone back home," you said with cautious, misplaced hopefulness.

The look that you and Kosey exchanged meant that you both didn't believe that.

"You better go before it's too late." Kosey stood up and picked up two items from a nearby shelf. He handed the first item to you, a simple white wallet-sized card with a single name, address, and phone number on it.

"This is our friend Arthur's contact details. When you are home and ready, call him and ask him to train you. Tell him I sent you."

Kosey then handed the second item to you. The object looked old, battered and was clamshell shaped. It was brass and reminded you of an old pocket watch. You pressed a button, and the lid popped up to reveal an antique compass.

You looked at Kosey quizzically, "What's this for?"

"This is to find your way to the Volta."

"I've got a compass on my phone; I can just use that, though. Can't I?"

"Modern phones or traditional maps will only be able to get you part of the way there. When you get lost and you will. Hopelessly so. Take this compass out, and when it spins, you've found them."

"What the hell does that mean?"

"You'll see," Kosey answered with a conspiratorial wink.

*

So, with the card and the compass safely in your pocket, you were soon queuing up to get on the plane for Khartoum.

Feeling uneasy and paranoid, you kept looking over your shoulder for Sean. Even when you were on the plane, and up in the air, you walked up and down the aisle looking for your stalker.

When you felt confident enough that nobody was following you anymore, you sat down to enjoy the rest of the flight.

The flight to Khartoum was a relatively short three hours. you spent most of it checking in with Vasia.

You told her the entire story about what happened with Kosey, being followed by Sean and being shot and everything. When Vasia heard about you getting shot, she insisted on you and her Facetime each other. Before the call, you put your earbuds in to keep as much of the conversation private as possible.

"Are you sure you're ok?" She immediately asked.

"Yes, I'm fine," you reassured her.

"Who do you think this Sean person is?"

"He said he was from Counter-Terrorism at Scotland Yard. I have a feeling those two detectives that came to our house the other day sent him."

"I thought I saw them at the airport but thought nothing of it."

Something in the sound of Vasia's voice and the look on her face caused a horrible feeling deep down in your gut that she might not be telling you everything.

"Well, be careful," you said to her, "Don't want to scare you, but they might want to follow you, so keep an eye out."

"Don't worry about me," Vasia said with a laugh that felt forced, "I've got my panic alarm with me if anything happens."

Partly out of guilt, but mostly out of protectiveness over Vasia, you asked, "Do you want me to come back home? I can get the next plane if need be."

"No, don't you dare. I can handle myself. You need to find out what is going on with you."

"Ok." you reluctantly backed down.

Rather conveniently, Vasia changed the subject. "By the way, you have mail here. I've opened one. I hope you don't mind."

On the inside, you rolled your eyes and mused, not for the first time that nothing is private when you're married.

"It is a letter from that DIY retailer based in Milton Keynes. They want to invite you to an interview, and they have mentioned some times and dates for you to choose from within the next three weeks. They just need you to call and confirm."

"Ok text me the number, and I'll call them in a bit."

After you both said your goodbyes and love yous and hung up, Vasia texted you the number, as promised, and you phoned it to arrange an interview.

For the last couple of days since the motorway accident, you hadn't thought about being unemployed. Your mind had been so up in the air and spinning with the fact that you have superpowers. Talking about interviews again, rudely brought you back down to Earth.

*

Eventually, the plane touched down in Khartoum, and after you passed through passport control and security and picked up your blue Eurohike rucksack from the baggage claim, you hired a car from the airport's car hire desk.

The car was a new, black, Dacia Sandero Stepway. As soon as you got in you marveled at that new car smell and its clean black interior with it's built in sat nav. You were soon navigating through the bustling, hot, dusty, exotic streets of Khartoum and was appreciating the car's fully functioning aircon in the forty-degree Celsius heat.

At one point, you drove over Victory Bridge, crossing the River Nile and had to stop at a layby to admire the view.

Standing here, as someone who had never been to Sudan before, you mused at how the place was not how you expected it to be. From television and media, they paint the picture of Sudan as mostly desert. And a lot of it is. However, here in Khartoum, it was a busy, modern and vibrant metropolis with well-maintained roads that put the UK's pothole-ridden road network to shame.

Behind you, there were tall, imposing colourful buildings, including one white and blue building that housed the Central Bank of Sudan. There was another concrete and glass building called the GNPOC Tower. You later learned this was the country's oil and gas company.

There was also an impressive looking building in the not so far distance. It was in the shape of a ship's sail and was enormous; it loomed over most of the other buildings around it. This was the infamous, very prestigious Corinthia Hotel.

In front of you across from the magnificent and vast River Nile, you could see the Al Sunat Forest. An urban forest reserve and bird sanctuary, its luscious green trees and wildlife contradicted the surrounding buildings.

After a while, you reluctantly stopped your procrastinating. You could have admired this view all day, with the scorching sun shining, making everything that little bit more beautiful. But you knew you had somewhere to go.

Reluctantly you got back in your hire car and drove on.

Soon you had left the city, and after a while, the towns and villages you were passing were getting fewer the further you travelled. Eventually, after two hours driving, the road disappeared entirely, replaced by nothing but desert as far as the eye could see. The car's sat nav didn't recognise where you were, it kept telling you to make a u-turn and go back. You eventually switched the sat nav off and carried on through the desert with sand kicking up in the car's wake.

You were driving for almost three hours until you stopped and decided to get out to flex your legs.

As you exited the car, the sun's blistering heat slammed into you. The slight breeze offered no relief, barely colder than the sand. Despite this, you were barely sweating.

You got a map of Sudan that you brought from the airport and spread it out on the car bonnet to get my bearings. You pulled out your smartphone, too, and brought up the compass app. Suspicious that the compass app wasn't working correctly, you pulled out the antique compass that Kosey had given you and compared the two. The North was in a different direction.

"That is weird," you muttered to yourself, shaking your head.

You put your phone back in your pocket and decided to follow the antique compass. You climbed back in the car and carried on driving.

After another three hours, the drive was becoming very challenging. You were travelling up and down many monstrous dunes that were really putting the four-wheel-drive through its paces. After a while, the dunes disappeared, and you were traversing across a vast empty expanse of wasteland. It was so dry that the ground was full of cracks and jagged potholes. Saying that there had been no rain here for several months was probably a trifle optimistic.

The going was very bumpy. You were being jostled around in your seat. Occasionally you whacked your head on the car roof and swore like a trooper. If you hadn't had your super healing, you would have surely been knocked out.

The car's suspension put up a good fight, but after a while, there was a sickening metallic crashing noise. A big almighty bang followed it before smoke suddenly started coming up from the front of the car and it came to an undramatic stop.

You immediately got out of the car and popped the hood to have a look. This was for appearance's sake really because you were no car mechanic. However, you didn't need to be one to know that the engine smoking and having part of the undercarriage ripped away and laying on the dry hot ground behind the car was bad.

"Shit, well that's my deposit gone," you swore to herself as you looked on helplessly.

Thinking about what to do next, it suddenly occurred to you how lonely and quiet it was standing in the middle of this dry, sweltering desert wasteland under the blistering sun, with the only transport for miles around, kaput.

It was still hot as hell, that you were aware of, but it still didn't seem to affect you. There was not a bead of sweat on your forehead. You absentmindedly took a swig of water from your bottle.

After several moments of coming to terms with the loneliness and the feeling of desperation that occurs when your car breaks down, you shrugged your shoulders and said to yourself, "Oh well. I better get moving." Alone in the barren landscape, your voice sounded weird.

You retrieved your rucksack out of the car boot, put it on, and locked the car up. As the car lights flashed to confirm it was locked, you thought it was a pointless exercise in this vast wasteland with nobody else around.

You consulted the antique compass, and with your shoes throwing up dust as you went, you started across the vast wasteland towards the Volta.

Some time later, you were getting bored with walking. Thinking about what Kosey had said earlier about the potential to run faster, you started jogging.

The jogging increased in speed until, with a heavy rucksack on your back in the burning sun of the dry, sweltering desert, you were running like *Usain Bolt*, kicking up a trail of sand behind you.

You tried to push yourself harder. It took a few moments, but you started feeling that familiar feeling of primordial power coursing up your body from your feet to your head. As this feeling grew, blue sparks of electricity started swirling around you.

The electric swirls distracted you. So it was a surprise even to yourself, when a surge of speed shot you onwards like a literal bullet out of a gun.

"Oh shit!" Stunned, you weren't ready for it. Because of that, seconds later, you tripped and lost your balance.

You rolled over multiple times on the hard-baked ground. Your backpack, phone, and compass went flying in all directions.

Eventually, you skidded face first to a stop leaving a skid mark almost a mile long.

For a few moments, you laid motionless on the ground. You lifted your head spitting out sand. Cuts and friction burns covered your face. You didn't have to worry for long. You could feel you skin stitching itself as it quickly healed.

"Wow," you said to yourself as you rolled over onto your back.

You stood up, brushed the sand off yourself, and shook your head to get the sand out of your hair.

It took a few minutes, but you located all your belongings. Before securing your phone in the rucksack you ensured the Bluetooth was on, running app was ready and your wireless earbuds were in your ears. You tied the compass around your neck, making sure the straps were tight.

"Let's try this again," you dared yourself.

You kneeled on one leg down in the traditional starting block sprinters' stance. Looking straight ahead, hands in the dry sand, the primordial power feeling coursed through your body until the blue sparks of electricity started swirling around your body again.

You could feel your body wanting to propel forward. You tried to resist for as long as possible. But then you let go. The world seemed to blur around you making it impossible to gage yourself.

"WHOOOOOO... HOOOOOOOO," you cried, exhilarated, as you zoomed across the wasteland.

Moments later the fitness app said in its monotone voice, "Distance, 80 miles. Speed, 630 miles per hour. 645. 667…."

"Holy shit," you cried.

You felt like you could go faster!

At some point, the barren wasteland disappeared, and you were racing across white sand, and up and down massive dunes throwing sand at least 35 feet into the air. in your wake.

Still running, you consulted the antique compass. The needle that had been pointing north was now pointing in the opposite direction.

Frowning, disappointed that you couldn't enjoy your new found speed for a little bit longer, you skidded to a stop.

A good thing too because the soles of your shoes were smoking.

Switching the fitness app off but noting that you had run over 100 miles in five minutes first, you turned around and went back the way you had come. This time at a gentle jog.

You came to the foot of a high mountainous dune. You climbed it, and when you got to the top, you looked around. Still nothing but desert. The compass needle had changed direction again. It was pointing the opposite way, so you had to climb down again.

"What the hell," you mumbled when you got back down to the bottom of the dune. Again, you consulted the compass. Once more, it was pointing back the way you had come.

You went up a few steps, keeping a wary eye on the compass the whole time.

The needle moved minutely to the east

You moved eastwards

The needle moved to the southwest

You took a few steps in that direction

The needle moved again to the north.

It carried on making minute changes like this, and you followed whatever direction the compass was telling you to go.

If anyone were watching, they would think you were trying to do some kind of Irish step dance.

Suddenly, the needle started spinning uncontrollably.

Confused, you looked down and around. There was nothing here.

You looked at the compass again. You swore the spinning needle was picking up speed. It was also glowing white.

The white glow gradually increased in size and enveloped you.

"What the…"

Had anyone been watching, they would have seen the white glow suddenly pulsate, and then you disappeared.

Chapter 24

"... hell," you finished as you materialised.

Instead of a sandy desert, there were tall, brown trees and lush, green vegetation everywhere. Birds were flying about singing. It was sunny, but there was a gentle cool breeze. The sun was getting low, and where it was kissing the horizon, there were flickers of red in the clouds, indicating that there will be a beautiful, glorious sunset within the next hour.

To your left in the not so far distance, there was a fenced meadow with horses grazing.

To your right, there was a prominent Georgian house with various people going to and from it. The scene was so surreal that you thought you were dreaming. If you didn't know any better, you could have been on any country farm back in England. Except for the fact Ermee and Eraaf were standing in front of you. And what they said to you.

Smiling, Ermee stepped forward, "Hello, Simon. Welcome to the Volta."

"Did you just beam me up somewhere?" was the first thing your dazed mind could think to say

"No, we're still in the desert," Ermee said as she and Eraaf directed you towards the Georgian house.

"Our tiny village is, how do I put it, 'cloaked' from the outside world and that little compass in your hand allows you to find your way through that cloak."

"Why are you cloaked?" you asked.

"That's a long story, one that we will tell you during dinner around a campfire tonight. For now, though, let's freshen up."

When you got to the house, Ermee mounted the steps and went in, followed by Eraaf who up till now had remained quiet. He turned to you staring for a moment that was verging on uncomfortable. Eventually, he bowed his head before turning back around and going into the house.

You felt like you should say something to Eraaf's retreating back.

"You know why I've come, don't you?" It was more of a statement than a question. "Will you tell me what I need to know?"

Eraaf did not stop but over his shoulder he mumbled one word.

"Dinner."

After a few moments, you shrugged. That wasn't exactly the answer you wanted but you were hungry. So you followed the two tribes-people into the house.

*

A little while later, you had changed into fresh clothes complete with a black hoodie as it was getting decidedly cooler now that that night time had descended.

With Ermee, Eraaf and several other people from the Xuholo tribe, you were sitting in the middle of the meadow. The horses had been stabled.

The only light was coming from the roaring campfire that everyone was sitting around in a big circle.

One of the female tribes-people handed everyone bowls of some kind of soup made from various herbs and spices. You gladly took the dish. It was a good thing you were hungry. The soup was off some indescribable colour and texture that would have usually caused you to lose your appetite. You, however, showed your appreciation by immediately devouring it. To be honest, after the first mouth full, you fell in love with the sweet flavoursome taste and had finished eating it before anyone else. It left you with a warm, fuzzy, tingly feeling.

As everybody else finished their soup, Eraaf, who was sitting on the opposite side of the fire from you spoke.

The entire time his eyes were transfixed on you. The reflection of the dancing flames in his eyes took on a haunting look.

Eraaf started off by talking about the history of the Xuholo tribe.

"From the dawn of time, our people have always been around. In this desolate desert wasteland part of the world, cut off from the rest of the world we flourished, and while everybody else was still stuck in the stone age, we were the most advanced civilization on Earth with advancements in technology that are still enviable by today's standards.

"We were only a tiny village like we are today, but we had the greatest and strongest economy that anybody had ever seen. But because we were unseen by the rest of the world, no one knew it. We were superior in every aspect; we had the greatest economists, the greatest scholars, the greatest scientists, even the greatest sorcerers that the world never knew. The only thing we were missing was a defence force.

For several millennia, we were allowed to flourish, oblivious to what was happening in the outside world. That was until the likes of the Egyptian and Persian empires came knocking on our door. They discovered us, and they all wanted a part of us, mainly our technology, which they found out could be used to turn into powerful weapons.

Because we didn't have a defence force of any kind, we could only sit back or get slaughtered as these invaders from foreign empires tried to seize our technology. We quickly saw the devastation that this would all cause and we didn't want any part of it. So, our greatest minds got together and quickly invented the cloak that you see protecting our village today. It was then that we disappeared from the rest of the world.

However, now that we had had a brief glimpse of the outside world, we ventured out to explore and get a greater understanding of it. We wanted to see if the rest of the world were like the Egyptian and Persians. And to some extent the Romans. What we found both horrified and delighted us. Yes, much of the world was split by empires that waged senseless, bloody and horrific wars on each other for nothing more than strips of territory or to force their culture or religion on others. As the centuries wore on the wars only got more bloody and even more horrific.

Very early on in our exploration, we quickly realised that the world would never be ready for our knowledge and technology, and we agreed to keep it a secret. However, amid all this fighting and carnage, we came across individuals who showed they had the same principles as us and were worthy of being bestowed all our knowledge and power. In return, we just asked that they don't tell anyone about us, and to protect people as and when people need help in a way that doesn't draw attention to them or us."

As Eraaf continued with his story, you stared transfixed into the fire. You could see Eraaf's story playing out in the flames.

After a while, you lost your concentration. You didn't mean to. Your head was becoming fuzzy. You felt like you would go to sleep for the first time in over a week. As you drifted off, your last thought was, "Damn, someone must have put something in that soup."

You had only closed your eyes for a brief second when you felt a rush of icy air, and a feeling akin to falling. Almost like that feeling you get when you're about to go to sleep, and your body jumps.

You immediately opened your eyes and found you were still sitting in front of the campfire with Eraaf directly opposite staring at you.

"Where's everybody gone?" You asked, looking around panicked noticing it was just you two.

"Everybody is still here," Eraaf answered enigmatically, "I am now conversing with you on a higher plane of existence."

"You did put something in my soup, didn't you?" you said, skeptically.

Eraaf ignored your comment.

"You came here to find out who you are, right?" Eraaf made it a statement rather than a question.

"Yes, what is happening to me? How did I get these powers?"

"I gave them to you," Eraaf answered, even more, cryptic than before.

"Why?"

"We only give powers to those that we deem worthy."

Unsatisfied by the answer but realizing you needed to approach this a different way, you claimed, "But I don't think I am worthy. You say as a rule you like to stay secret and keep to the shadows, but I think I might have already broken that rule."

"Ah, you mean the day on the motorway," Eraaf mentioned.

"Yes." And then, slightly confused, you asked, "How do you know about that?"

"I see everything," Eraaf answered mysteriously. "Plus, we have TV here."

"See, so you know I've put you in danger."

"Nothing that we can't handle, none of the pictures or videos taken got a clear shot of your face, and people will forget about it by next week, anyway. The only thing you need to worry about is your country's authorities."

"Exactly, someone claiming they are from Counter-Terrorism was following me and shot me twice and saw me heal both times. They may have followed my wife as well, but she's not sure. It will only be a matter of time before they come after me."

"They might or they might not," Eraaf said with frustrating calmness, "If they do, you will be ready for it."

"I don't think I will be," you disagreed. "I have no idea how to use these superpowers. I don't know what I can do."

"You know more than you think."

"You're just a fountain of cryptic one-liners aren't you," you bit back sarcastically.

Eraaf raised an eyebrow, the only sign that your comment slightly vexed him.

"You have the potential to be the most powerful person on this planet, and you have already begun to realise that potential. You have learnt that you are immortal, you can heal very quickly, you have visions of the future, you have super strength, and just before you got here, you discovered you have super speed. You will soon realise that you can do anything if you put your mind to it. You can even fly."

"But I can't control any of it. Plus, I don't think I can fly."

"That comes with experience. Now you're like a child learning to ride a bike. The stabilisers have come off, and you're wobbling and falling all over the place. But soon you learn to balance and after a while, riding a bike becomes second nature to you."

"Yeah but if we use your child on a bike analogy, there's usually an adult helping them, and I need help."

Seeming to decide, Eraaf immediately stood up with a speed that shouldn't be possible for an elderly man, and made you flinch. He walked around the campfire with his wooden staff saying, "I have another analogy. Before the caterpillar goes in the cocoon, he does not know that he can do what a butterfly does. But when he becomes a butterfly, he has all the knowledge of a butterfly." Eraaf stopped in front of you, and you hurriedly stood up to face Eraaf.

"You will now go into your cocoon and will have all the knowledge of a butterfly when you come out." Eraaf's staff started glowing orange.

He lifted it up, and before you could think to object, he touched your forehead with it. Your body immediately stiffened, and you fell, unstoppable, to the ground like a tree. Your entire body the colour of grey.

Chapter 25

In some other plane of existence, you found yourself alone in an empty, nondescript, bright white room of indescribable size.

"Holy crap, I'm in *The Matrix*!"

A few yards away, you noticed a stone pillar that you were sure wasn't there a moment before. You went over to it and saw that there was a simple red button on top. It had the words "Press Me" inscribed on it.

With some degree of trepidation you hesitated for a moment.

"Pressing a button just because it's telling me too is not going to lead to anything good." You said to yourself.

You pressed the button anyway.

The white room suddenly disappeared and was replaced by blue sky and clouds.

Below you, you could see the land of Sudan and its neighbours laid out like a map.

You felt freezing cold. It was unusually windy and cloudy. It took a few moments for you to figure that you were falling straight through these clouds towards the land below.

"CRAP!" You swore, Screaming you continued your uncontrollable spiralling descent. "ERAAF, HELP ME!"

Eraaf suddenly appeared in front of you. Inexplicably, he was sitting cross-legged, as if he was still at the campfire.

"When a butterfly comes out of its cocoon, it knows how to fly. So, fly," he said unhelpfully. he then disappeared as quickly as he had appeared.

"What?" "Are you crazy?" You asked the now empty space. "I can't fly. I don't know how TOOOOOO" you cried as you continued to plummet towards land.

"You do know how to fly," came Eraaf's disembodied voice. "You just have to think you can, and you will."

In desperation, you adopted the Superman pose, but down you continued to fall. You tried the pose a few times, but all it did was make you full faster. A sick, terrible feeling gripped you as the ground was getting nearer and nearer. Screaming you closed your eyes. You waited to splatter like a runny egg. But it never happened.

You opened your eyes again and discovered you were back up in the clouds. You were momentarily relieved, but it didn't last for long. As if in some *Looney Tunes* cartoon, you started falling again.

Again, all you could do was scream and try various poses to fly, but of course, none of the attempts succeeded.

You were about to hit the ground for a second time when you appeared in the clouds again. And down you fell for the third time.

Then a fourth time.

It wasn't until you were halfway down on the fifth attempt that Eraaf appeared to you, sitting cross-legged again.

"Think about how you felt when you discovered your super strength and speed. Remember that, and you will fly." And with that, he disappeared again.

"How did I feel? What does that mean?" You said more to yourself, as Eraaf wasn't there anymore.

You started thinking about all the other times you discovered your other superpowers and what you were doing.

Speaking to yourself again, you started counting down the times "That one time with Kosey it was because I was angry and I wanted him to stop so I pictured pushing him, the second time was because I wanted to run fast, so I pictured it, and I did it." The penny suddenly dropped, "Is that it? All I need to do is picture it, and I'll do it?"

Nobody answered.

Still falling and the ground getting nearer, in your mind's eye, you drew a picture of yourself flying and the familiar feeling of primordial power coursed through your body starting from your legs.

The ground was getting nearer and nearer.

The primordial power feeling rose from your legs until you felt it enveloping your entire body.

The ground was still getting nearer fast.

Sparks of electricity swirled around your body. Instead, this time the colour was white not the blue came with your super-speed.

You stopped falling. You looked down and saw that you were hovering just a few inches off the ground.

Not quite believing it, you chuckled deliriously. This time as you put your arms up in the Superman pose, you shot straight up in the air. Screaming with incoherent joy, you made a few loops de loops for good measure.

Your joy was short-lived. A few seconds later, you found yourself in the white room again.

You immediately stopped flying and dropped like a stone face first.

"Owww."

You picked yourself up, rubbing your nose.

Eraaf appeared beside you with a pop, making you jump.

Standing now, Eraaf declared, "Now you know how to fly. But more importantly, you know the secret of how to tap into your powers."

"So, all I have to do is think about it, and I can do it?" you asked, still not quite believing it. "Isn't that cheating?"

"No, just a major advantage."

Suddenly a thought occurred to you. "With all these powers, what is my weakness?"

It was Eraaf's turn to look confused.

"Well, *Superman's* weakness is Kryptonite, while *Green Lantern's* is anything yellow. *Spiderman* seems to lose his web shooter ammo at the most inconvenient time. With *Wolverine* it's magnets, *Bruce Willis* in *Unbreakable* is afraid of water," you explained.

"This is no superhero comic book movie. This is real life, don't think of it as such. You might have some weaknesses but hope that nobody finds out what it is."

"Hope that nobody finds out what it is," you echoed, incredulous. "That's not very helpful. If I don't know what my own weaknesses are, how do I stop other people from finding out?"

"That's exactly how nobody finds out. If you don't know, nobody can find out from you." And then thinking for a moment, Eraaf added, "If it makes you happy, you seem to have a big weakness for drugs."

"Why do you say that?"

"Well, you're tripping really bad at the moment after having that soup."

"See, I knew you put something in there!"

Changing the subject slightly, Eraaf added, "Before we finish our lesson for today you need to know that with your visions you can learn to control them, have them whenever you need them rather than them coming to you at some inconvenient time. Also, with time you will learn to expand the time frame of when your vision is based in years into the future."

"Can I use it to see next week's lottery numbers?"

"You shouldn't use your powers for personal gain," Eraaf admonished.
You picked up on Eraaf's language. "I noticed you said 'shouldn't' not couldn't."

"I advise against it."

"Fair enough," you said, thinking better than to push it anymore.

"You must remember now that you have to be responsible…"

"I know, I know," you interrupted. "With great power, comes great responsibility and all that crap."

"No," Eraaf said, looking a bit deflated. "I was going to say; responsibility is not about happiness, and it's not in impulsive decisions."

"Well, that's boring," you said, disappointed. "Did someone say that?"

"I might have paraphrased some Canadian psychologist. Anyway, getting back on topic, you need to know that you can have a vision whenever you want."

"How do I do that? Do I just think about it?"

"Give it a go."

For a while, you just stood there, trying hard to think about having a vision. You rubbed your temples, hoping that would help.

Eventually, Eraaf broke the silence, "You just look like you're constipated!"

"It's no use, I don't know how to start a vision," you mumbled, defeated.

"What were you doing before when you had your visions?"

"I don't know, not much. The first time, I was lying in bed in hospital, the second time I was having a pee in a pub toilet, and then the last time I was on my computer, job hunting."

"So, would you say you weren't thinking about anything in particular? What you just described you do multiple times a day without having to think about it. A kind of trance produced by the monotony of the everyday."

"I guess so."

"So, you might have to do the exact opposite of what you normally do when you tap into your powers. Empty your mind of all thoughts."

"You mean I have to meditate?"

"You can try it, but I doubt you need to go that far."

"Ok, so just empty my mind, don't think of anything," you said. "I think I can do that. My wife says I'm not much of a thinker anyway." you added with a nervous chuckle, "How hard can it be?"

Standing there in the middle of the endless white room with Eraaf looking on, you tried to force yourself to empty your head of all thoughts. Suffice to say after a few minutes of rubbing your temples with your eyes closed repeating to yourself, "Empty my head of all thoughts", repeatedly, you eventually gave up.

"It's no use," you claimed frustrated. "All I can do is think now."

"Ok, you're frustrated, you're trying to force the issue. Let's try meditation. Sit down."

You and Eraaf sat down opposite each other, crossed-legged in the middle of the white room. The bonfire from the meadow suddenly appeared between you. You rocked back in surprise more from the appearance of the fire than from the sudden heat. Eraaf remained his usual tranquil calm self.

"Right I want you to look into the fire, feel the heat, hear the crackling. Do you feel the heat?"

"I do," you answered staring into the fire, the reflection of the flames dancing in your eyes.

"Do you hear the crackling?"

"I do," you answered again.

You could already feel yourself becoming mesmerised by the dancing flames and the cosy warm heat.

"What are you thinking about right now?"

"About how crazy it is sitting here," you replied smartly.

"Anything else?"

My thoughts drifted.

"About how Vasia will think about how crazy I am when I tell her this story, later."

"And is there anything else about your wife you're thinking of?"

You paused for a moment which prompted Eraaf to ask, "Is there anything on your mind, that's troubling you?"

"Yes, there is something actually."

"What is it?"

"Well, it's been niggling at the back of my mind since I met Kosey in Cairo. I'm immortal, right?"

Eraaf nodded with a knowing smile on his face.

"What about my wife?" you asked with an emotional frown.

"What about her?" Eraaf unhelpfully answered with another question.

"Well, I'm immortal, but she's not. Which means she will grow old and die someday. And I won't."

"How does that make you feel?"

His question forced you to face your emotions. The one thing men aren't adept at.

"I don't know. A lot of things. Sad because I love her. Scared because I don't want to be without her. Angry. Frustrated because why can't she be immortal as well or why can't I be mortal. All the above."

"I see," was all Eraaf said, with insane calmness.

"Also," you added, your voice quivering slightly, "Confused. As in why this happened to me?"

"I see you have a lot of feelings and questions. What I want you to do for now is picture those feelings and those questions and push them into the fire until you can visualise them in there."

"Ok, I think I can do that," you said, sounding unsure.

"So, take your feeling of sadness, visualise it in your mind and push it into the fire. "Then take your feelings of fear and visualize them pushed into the fire, Eraaf said in a calm, monotone voice.

And you did just that; You took each feeling and pushed them into the fire.

For some inexplicable reason, your imagination was visualising your feelings as children dressed in Victorian clothing. They were linked arm in arm, forming a big circle with yourself and Vasia in the middle, cuddling each other. The children were laughing and dancing and singing the *'Ring around the roses'* nursery rhyme.

As a complete polar opposite to the children's laughter, the Simon and Vasia in the circle were looking thoroughly miserable, as if the circle of children they were in was actually some kind of prison.

"Now whatever you see, I want you to concentrate on the sound of the crackling fire," Eraaf said. "Concentrate on it, find the rhythm in it, as if you are listening to a song. Immerse yourself in it, sway to the sound."

You were conscious of the popping and snapping of the crackling fire.

"Feel the heat of the fire," Eraaf continued "Let the warmth wash over you."

You felt the warmth radiating off the fire. It felt like it was wrapping you in some big woolly snuggly blanket.

You were feeling dozy. The laughing and dancing children and the miserable Simon and Vasia in the fire faded away.

"Now see the flames," Eraaf carried on saying in that same calm monotone, "Watch the flames as they wave and pulsate. Watch the flames as they lick and flow over the burnt wood. Watch the flames as they weave in and out of the image you have just conjured."

You sat, looking mesmerised into the fire. The flames took on some kind of hypnotic component as you carried on watching the fading scene in the fire.

Eraaf repeated, "Watch the flames as they wave and pulsate. Watch the flames as they lick and flow over the burnt wood. Watch the flames as they weave in and out of the image you have just conjured."

He repeated the same mantra several times, each time his voice calmed more from the time before, and each time the image faded more and more from the fire until it finally disappeared.

Moments later, there was an unceremonious pop. Eraaf and everything else disappeared.

Chapter 26

You found yourself sitting on a soft grey carpet.

Looking around, it took a few seconds for your brain to believe what your eyes were telling you.

"What the hell am I doing back home?" You wondered out aloud to yourself. You were sitting cross-legged in the middle of your living room.

It was daytime. The sun was shining pleasantly through the windows and the open sliding patio backdoor.

From your viewpoint, you could see into the back garden. It was small, mostly grass, with half of it taken over by a seven by seven-foot wooden shed. There were half a dozen potted hanging baskets with colourful plants that you didn't know the names of. Vasia was the gardener of the house.

Against the side of the shed was a concrete post almost the same height as the shed itself. Tied to the concrete post was a washing line that stretched back to the house. On the washing line were various bits of damp laundry that Vasia, at this moment in time, was hanging.

You stood up and watched Vasia as she finished putting the washing on the line.

Standing at the door, you called to Vasia, but she didn't hear you.

She picked up the now empty plastic basket and started towards the house.

At that moment, there was a knock at the door. You turned and looked down the hallway to the front door. Through the frosted glass that made up the top half of the door, all you could make out were three black shapes.

For some inexplicable reason, those shapes made the hairs on the back of your neck stand up. You did not like the look of this.

Vasia stepped into the house and made her way to the front door.

Unfortunately, you were standing in the way. This didn't stop her. She didn't seem to see you, she walked straight through you and there was that icy sensation you felt back at the pub the other night. Your body shimmered as she went through. You yelped in surprise.

You quickly shook off your surprise and followed Vasia to the front door.

"Don't open the door Vasia. I've got a nasty feeling about this," you said to her. But off course she couldn't hear you.

However, when she got to the door, she left the chain on as she opened it. Peering through the gap that the chain allowed, she saw three people dressed all in black with balaclavas over their heads. Two of them had Sig Sauer P229 pistols holstered at the hip but the third one, nearest the door, was carrying a Heckler & Koch MP5SF semi-automatic assault rifle. The person had the gun unholstered with the muzzle end, pointing to the ground.

Despite the intimidating sight, Vasia, with a calmness that was hiding the suspicion and growing fear she felt inside, said, "Um, yes?"

"Is Simon Emerson here?" said the person with the rifle. He was presumably a man on account of his butch Essex accent.

"No, he's out," Vasia said, slightly nervous.

"Are you Vasia Emerson?"

"Yes, what is this about?"

At this point, the guy lifted the muzzle of his rifle and pointed it straight at Vasia's head through the open gap, "Let us in," he growled.

"Umm, no." Vasia quickly shut the door, and backed away from it.

The man with the rifle gave the door a swift hard kick, and it burst open, putting stress on the hinges. It was on the chain still, so all that happened was that it rattled and slammed shut again.

Still, this made Vasia scream and jump in fear. Her hands shaking, she got her phone out of her pocket and dialled 999.

"I'm calling the police," she shouted defiantly to the masked people behind the door.

You were facing Vasia.

"Quick, go out the back!" you shouted at her.

The rifleman, ignoring Vasia's warning, gave the door another swift kick, but the chain held.

With her mobile to her ear, hearing the familiar click on the other end of the phone to signify that someone was picking up, Vasia shouted, "I'm warning you; I am speaking to the police now."

"Emergency," a soft female voice with a Liverpudlian accent answered, "What service do you require? Fire, Police or Ambulance?"

"Police, please," Vasia answered in a panicked tone. Then she screamed. A natural response to the rifleman smashing the frosted glass with the butt of his gun and reaching in with a black leather-gloved hand to unchain the door.

Seemingly taking your advice, Vasia, wasting no more time, turned to run back down the hallway and through the living room.

As she turned to run, the emergency operator, on hearing Vasia scream, calmly asked, "Is your life in danger?"

"Yes, it is!" Vasia shouted, nearly hysterical, as she ran, "Men are trying to break into my house."

"Ok," the operator carried on professionally. "We know where you are, we have got your address by pinging your mobile phone, and we have dispatched a police car to your location. Now try to get to a safe place and hide."

"I'm trying," Vasia practically screamed as she entered the back garden.

Behind her, Rifleman had unchained the door, and the three of them came running in, with their guns drawn.

For all the good it would do, you tried standing in their way, but all three ran straight through you.

Making the mistake of looking behind her, Vasia tripped and fell awkwardly to the grass, her phone flew out of her hand and landed, display-side up, a few inches away.

The men made quick work of running through the house and out into the back garden. They quickly caught up to Vasia before she could pick herself up from the ground.

The two men with the Sig Sauers grabbed Vasia. One of them holstered his gun, lifted Vasia over his shoulder in a fireman's lift and proceeded to carry her kicking and screaming back through the house and out through the front door.

However, your typical damsel in distress, Vasia wasn't.

Years ago Vasia and some friends attended many ladies only self-defence classes to support one friend in the group after someone had attacked them while walking home late at night. Vasia had passed the courses with frightening ease and had the certificates to prove it.

Therefore, Vasia knew how to stand up for herself.

The man hadn't even taken a step when he collapsed to his knees in pain from a well-placed nerve pinch on the muscle connecting the back of the guy's head to the shoulder.

She broke out of the guy's grip, and while he was still kneeling on the ground, she turned to him with a look of unrelenting determination on her face and kicked him right in the crown jewels. The man fell to the ground in the fetal position, choking on his own pain.

"Woo-hoo, way to go Vasia!" you shouted. Feeling like a cheerleader, all you could do was stand on the sidelines. Then urgently you shouted, "Watch out."

The second man with the Sig Sauer was advancing on Vasia from behind. She seemed to sense this, pivoted on her left foot and rotating her hips, she lifted her elbow to shoulder height and struck the guy in the face. He staggered back, dazed.

Turning to face the second man proper, and before he could shake his dizziness off, with her dominant hand, she used her palm and aimed for the attacker's nose. There was a definite cracking sound as blood gushed out of his nose saturating his balacava. His nose now broken, his eyes rolled up in his head and he groaned before falling to the floor like a massive oak tree.

"Damn, maybe I should ask Vasia to train me to fight," you said as you looked on with a mixture of surprise and pride.

Just as the second man fell to the ground, the third grabbed Vasia from behind in a bear hug.

Reflexively, Vasia wasted no time stomping his foot and using the back of her head to bash him in the face.

Screaming in pain, the man let go to hold his nose.

Vasia turned to the man and was about to punch him when there was a faint clicking noise, and she suddenly stopped. Her whole body went rigid. Her eyes opened wide, she seemed to be stuck in an eternal look of surprise.

A second later, she fell to the ground and started convulsing. The two metal prongs sticking out of her back were traced back to something neither of you had noticed.

A fourth person stood slightly behind you.

"Where the hell did you come from?" You asked.

Also dressed all in black and with a balaclava over his face, this one was holding an object that looked very much like a gun. It was black with a stripe of yellow at the muzzle end. From your viewpoint, you could see the word PULSE+ embossed on the barrel of the gun, and two wires were protruding out of it, leading to the metal prongs sticking out of Vasia's back. It was emitting quick brief flashes of light and a low clicking noise.

Dismayed, you realized Vasia was getting tasered.

The fourth man only had his finger on the trigger for a maximum of five seconds, but when he took his finger off, Vasia went limp. It looked like she had lost consciousness.

"Now," said the fourth man in a familiar Cockney accent, "Do you think you can handle her?" he added with heavy hints of sarcasm and derision.

The other three who all looked battered and bruised, or bloodied, or all of the above, nodded sheepishly.

The first one who had received a kick in the crown jewels gingerly got back up on his feet. After checking to make sure they were still attached and presumably in working order, he awkwardly lifted Vasia on his shoulder in a fireman's lift.

This time there was no trouble from her, apart from a few groans to show she was just stunned and not unconscious as you first thought. He carried her back through the house and out through the front door. The other three followed closely behind.

You tried to stand in their way, desperately shouting for them to stop but that didn't do any help.

Out the front door and on the street, there was a brand new black Range Rover with black-tinted windows sitting idle.

Still stunned and unresponsive they lifted Vasia into the back and positioned her in the middle with two of the balaclava-wearing men sitting either side of her. The third man with the rifle sat shotgun, and the fourth man with the stun gun got into the driver's seat.

Without bothering to check if his passengers had their seat belts on, they sped off with a roar of the V8 engine and a screech of tyres.

Screaming for the men to give back your wife, you tried to chase after the Range Rover, but it was soon round the corner and out of sight.

Screaming now at empty space, there was a sudden pop, and you were suddenly somewhere else.

Momentarily confused and distraught over Vasia's kidnapping, you frantically looked about to get your bearings.

"What the fuck is this?" you asked yourself desperately

At first, all you could see was people, hundreds upon hundreds of people. You were in fact standing in the middle of a sea of noisy, happy, determined-looking people.

Most of them were wearing running gear. On the odd occasion some, for some inexplicable reason, were wearing various kinds of costumes. There were animal costumes, superhero costumes, cartoon character costumes. There was even someone dressed up as Big Ben!

You noticed that everyone was wearing a piece of paper with a black number pinned to their fronts. You looked down at yourself, and you were wearing one too. Complete with your green Karrimor running top, black shorts and blue trainers.

You would not have had a clue as to your whereabouts if it wasn't for some familiar landmarks. Not far away from where you were standing, over the sea of people, you could just make out the infamous white dome of Greenwich Royal Observatory. A little further from that was the familiar towering sails of the Cutty Sark.

Even further away on the near horizon, you could make out the London Eye and various tower blocks.

With the thousands of people and the music blaring out on gigantic speakers, you would have been forgiven for thinking you were at some massive street party if it wasn't for what you saw in front of you.

"Holy shit." you said as the penny dropped "I'm at the London Marathon."

About 300 yards up towering above the crowd there was a makeshift bridge. They made the dome of the bridge up with hundreds of white and red balloons with a big red banner with the Virgin Money logo on it. On the legs on both sides of the bridge, there were the words 'Virgin Money London Marathon' and the year. Underneath in smaller lettering, for the twitterphiles of us was written #LondonMarathon.

With everyone chatting excitedly, the noise was almost unbearable, but it subsided a bit as a female voice started talking over a loudspeaker.

"Thank you, everybody, for coming." She started. "In a matter of minutes, the marathon will begin."

You felt the excited buzz in the air increase tenfold.

The lady carried on talking, instructing what would happen next.

You zoned out a bit as you continued to look around at the faces of people taking part. A few metres away, there was a metal barrier. Behind the barricade, there were spectators who all seemed to be excited to see the marathon start as much as the participants were.

There was one runner, an athletic-looking female standing beside the barrier talking to a man and a three-year-old toddler on the other side of the barricade who was presumably her husband and son. Despite the awkwardness of the barrier, the three of them were taking selfies as they hugged and kissed each other.

Seeing this, you couldn't help but smile, and you were about to turn away when you saw something out of the corner of your eye.

With the vast crowd it was surprising you even noticed, but when you looked back around, you confirmed it. You definitely saw it.

A figure, carrying a nondescript navy-blue backpack, was marching purposefully straight through the crowd. He did not seem to notice or care about the spectators he was in the middle of or the runners behind the barrier. Dressed in black jeans and a dark green hoodie with the hood pulled up and over his head so it covered his face, you couldn't see who it was. But as soon as you clocked him you knew. This was the Green Park terrorist.

Breathing heavily, you stood fused to the spot for a few moments, seeming not to be able to move.

Just as the figure was about to disappear from eyesight, you spurred into action.

Moving as quickly as possible through hordes of runners, you leapt over the barriers.

You started after the figure, but your going wasn't easy considering the crowds of people.

The Green Hood suddenly changed direction and started heading towards the observatory where the crowd was a little thinner.

You changed direction, too, increasing your speed.

You momentarily lost sight of the Green Hood, when a knot of people, seemingly as one organism, walked straight into you. They were laughing and talking to each other and were oblivious to you, despite your cursing and shouting at them to get out the way.

Eventually, you got through to the other side of the group and caught sight of the Green Hood almost immediately. He was by a park bench kneeling as if he was tying a shoe but as you looked on; you saw the Green Hood fiddle with something in his backpack and then slide it under the park bench.

Wasting no time, you broke into a run and sprinted after the guy.

"Hey! Stop!" you shouted after him, but he paid no heed.

After sliding the backpack under the bench, he stood up and casually started walking towards the observatory with his hands in his pockets.

You had nearly caught up to him when the Green Hood walked around the edge of the building. He had only disappeared from view for a few seconds before you too rounded the corner.

You stopped. The Green Hood had disappeared.

There were people around sitting on the grass or walking towards the spectators. Apart from that, Greenwich Park was empty. It was like the Green Hood had disappeared into thin air.

You stood confused for a few moments wondering where the hell the hooded figure had gone. Then remembering the backpack, the Green Hood had put under one of the park benches, you turned and ran up to it.

At the park bench, you got to your knees, retrieved the backpack from underneath it and looked inside.

What you saw took your breath away. It took the entire space of the backpack up—a metal cylinder resembling a small beer barrel. Wires were protruding out of the cylinder into an object the size of a smartphone. On the screen of the object were numbers counting down.

As you looked on, you vaguely heard the announcer over the loudspeaker announcing that the marathon would start imminently and started counting down from ten.

You had the presence of mind to realise that the countdown timer on the bomb was counting down in parallel with the announcer over the loudspeaker.

"Ten... nine... eight," the announcer yelled over the speaker, and the runners and speakers joined in unison.

"Seven... six... five."

You immediately stood up and started yelling at everyone to run.

216

"Four... three... two."

"Everybody run!" you kept shouting, desperately running towards the hordes of spectators and runners.

"One... zero." And then the klaxon sounded for everyone to start the marathon.

"Oh no," you uttered in dismay.

Suddenly, you had a bird's eye view of the entire scene. Just as the klaxon sounded, there was an eruption of furious energy and radiation.

Pretty much everyone in Greenwich Park including yourself and the 40,000 plus runners in the queue to start the marathon didn't have time to register this as they were immediately engulfed in light and energy.

The initial release created an immense reaction of intense energy and heat that washed over the entire place like a wave. Within seconds anything it touched that was made of solid matter totally evaporated.

The wave of radiation and heat rolled on for miles. In the five to ten-mile radius, people and animals had the luck of having a few seconds to register the fact that a bomb exploded. But with the very air on fire, everybody and everything felt excruciating pain for just a split second. Their skin and muscle melted off their bodies, and they landed on the floor as black husks.

As the wave of radiation reached the ten to fifteen-mile radius, a secondary explosion radiated from the epicentre, sending a massive shock wave. Any building or landmark including, train stations, hospitals or structures of any kind both human-made or natural, including trees that stood in the way of the shock wave, were utterly obliterated.

Greenwich Park Observatory, Cutty Sark, The O2, Canary Wharf, The Tower of London. Even Buckingham Palace. All destroyed.

In fact, everything within a twenty-mile radius of Greenwich Park from Wembley Stadium in the east to the

Bluewater Shopping Centre in the west. From Waltham Abbey in the north and Clacket Lane Services on the M25 in the south, it destroyed every single building in a sea of fire.

Those people on the London Underground who survived the initial wave were not safe either as the shock wave of fire roared into the underground stations, down the escalators and through the tunnels, instantly evaporating any person standing there.

A mushroom cloud ascended several miles into the air which could be seen from as far away across the Channel in France.

Residents of Watford, Southend, Royal Tunbridge Wells and Harlow were close enough to have to shield their eyes from the blast and until the fallout came, some only experienced minor burns akin to a terrible sunburn.

*

You quickly sat up sweating and screaming as if you had come out of an exceptionally terrible nightmare. Disoriented, it took a few moments to realise you were still in the meadow. In front of you, the bonfire was now dead reduced to a lump of cold black and grey charcoal mess. Eraaf was sitting directly opposite staring at you with that same unnerving, patient, knowing smile of his.

It was daylight; the sun was shining high in the sky. you realised that you must have been on this trippy meditation vision thing all night!

"What did you see?" Eraaf asked calmly.

After getting your breath back, you told him about your two visions. As soon as you mentioned the bomb exploding, Eraaf's usually calm demeanour took on a noticeable serious edge.

"When is it going to happen?" he asked, concerned.

"Sunday, the day of the London Marathon."

Alert, Eraaf stood up. "You will have to go back now."

"Yeah, it will take a while to go back the way I came," you agreed, confused by the old man's sudden change in attitude.

"No, you will have to fly," Eraaf ordered.

Not catching on to Eraaf's meaning at first you started saying, "Why, have you got a plane you didn't tell me about?"

And then as the penny dropped.

"Oh, you mean fly," you punctuated the word "fly" by weaving your left arm across your body as an image of flying.

Eraaf nodded.

"Sure, I can do that," you said casually, as you stood up and brushed the dirt off your jeans, "But what's the hurry? It's not for a few days yet."

"No, it's today."

"What?"

"You have been in your meditative state for five days," Eraaf explained and then when you were still a bit slow on the uptake, "It's now Six am on Sunday in England. The London Marathon starts in four hours."

"Oh shit," you said your mind racing.

Chapter 27

You spent no time at all retrieving your backpack from inside the Georgian house and saying your goodbyes to everybody.

Minutes later, you were standing outside the house, talking to Eraaf and Ermee.

"Do you have any advice for me?" you asked Eraaf nervously as you struggled with adjusting the straps on your backpack.

"Don't fail," Eraaf answered pragmatically.

You stopped, looked at him, and wondered why he would say something like that.

"Thanks."

Ermee playfully punched Eraaf in the shoulder, feigning shock.

"What my grandfather means to say is that you can do it, we do not doubt it."

"Thanks," you said again then looked up at the sky, "I wish I had your confidence."

"That's just nerves speaking," Ermee said kindly. "You are more powerful than you think you are."

"Remember what I said before. You have powers that you don't even know you have," Eraaf added.

"And you have a kind heart. I see that" Ermee continued. "That's my superpower," she added, chuckling. "You will do everything you can to save everybody."

"I sure hope so," you said doubtfully then looked back to your mentor, "Well, I'm ready,"

After saying an awkward goodbye to the two tribes-people, you stepped back two steps.

Bending your legs slightly, you did a little jump and took off into the sky. It wouldn't occur to you until later you didn't have to do the Superman pose.

*

Initially shielding their eyes from the downdraft and then tracking Simon's trajectory, Eraaf's granddaughter asked: "Do you think he's ready?"

"He has to be," Eraaf answered, hoping that his confident tone masked what he was feeling.

"Should we help?"

"No, he needs to do this on his own."

"What happens when he finds out?"

"We'll deal with that when it comes."

*

You covered some 3500 miles to get back home in a quick time.

You flew just below the clouds where the air was cold and thin. But this didn't seem to affect you.

With no map, you found it easy to track where you were going by monitoring the geography. From this height, you didn't dare risk taking your smartphone out to use the GPS in case you dropped it.

Despite the urgency to get back, you allowed yourself to appreciate the craziness of the whole situation of this flying thing. You couldn't help but wonder at the beauty and awe of the views below either.

There were the pyramids of Egypt, and you recognised Cairo airport. You briefly wondered if Kosey was down there.

Next, you were flying over the beautiful Mediterranean where you came inches above the water so you could dip your hand in the chilly water. You were so engrossed in making ripples in the water and seeing your reflection that you almost didn't notice the big white cruise ship that was heading straight for you. With just a moment to spare, you looked up, saw it, and made a sharp, almost 90-degree turn straight up.

When you got high enough, you stopped and hovered in the sky, for a moment. Looking back down at the deck of the cruise ship there were people enjoying themselves walking about, playing games or sunbathing.

You were reasonably sure that you hadn't been made when an elderly couple sunbathing spotted you and started pointing excitedly. As you watched, the gentleman rushed over to one of the telescopes dotted around the edge of the deck. You decided it was a good idea to get out of there quick smart before the man could look through it.

Next, you were flying over the sun-baked Calabria region of Italy and followed the twisting road network through lush green forests and rugged mountains through to the Basilicata region with the beautiful City of Matara, famous for the vast hillside complex of cave dwellings.

Further on, you could see the intimidating and magnificent Mount Vesuvius with steam rising from within and the awe-inspiring ruins of Pompeii to the south and the beautiful city of Naples to the north.

After several moments you were flying over the snow peaks of the Swiss Alps, and with the highest of the mountains being three miles high, you just about skimmed the top of them. Finding it impossible to resist, you took a handful of snow as you went past.

From here you followed the road network through Switzerland, flying over the beautiful city of Zurich and the prominent picturesque lanes of the central Altstadt.

You looked down at the city, wishing you had enough time to go down. It was always on your bucket list to come here. You made a mental note to return another time with Vasia. It didn't escape your notice that you no longer had to pay for planes to travel somewhere. An enormous advantage especially with being out of a job.

Soon you had crossed the border into France and sprawled below were quaint little villages with medieval castles hidden in mountainous terrain. You could see many gorgeous looking vinyards with people picking the grapes.

Before you knew it, you were flying across the magnificent, imposing metropolis of Paris, crisscrossed by wide streets and the River Seine. You saw the twelfth century Gothic Notre-Dame Cathedral still being rebuilt after the great fire a few years back and the recognisable icon of the Eiffel Tower.

After Paris, you flew over the bustling port of Calais and then over the English Channel. It seemed busier than you expected with many cargo ships going to and from Dover and Calais. You could understand why the English Channel was one of the busiest shipping lanes in the world.

As soon as you saw the white cliffs of Dover, you felt a sense of emotional, patriotic pride well up inside, and the famous Vera Lynn song played in your head as you flew overhead.

"There'll be bluebirds over
The white cliffs of Dover
Tomorrow, just you wait and see…"

Not for the first time you wished you could stop just to take pictures.

From Dover, you followed the M20 into London and as you went over Greenwich, you stopped and hovered in the air for a few moments looking down at the scene below. It was almost the same vantage point from your vision. You were thinking about what was going to happen later, potentially.

You looked at your watch and noticed it was seven o'clock. The marathon would start in three hours. Already there were marshals dressed in high vis, busy working putting the finishing touches to it in the early morning spring sun. Some were sweeping and picking rubbish up, and some were putting barriers up, some were checking the sound system was working correctly. There were even several spectators and participants showing up and walking around aimlessly.

You were broken out of your reverie when you noticed several of these people looking up and pointing excitedly at you.

Despite being high up, you faintly heard one person asking; "Oi, what's that in the sky? Is it a person?"

"I don't know," a marshal said. "Let me get my binoculars from my car." The marshal ran off to his car to retrieve them.

Well, you weren't about to wait for him to retrieve them, so you promptly left toward home.

*

Back home in Luton, Vasia was finishing putting the laundry out on the washing line when she heard a thud from behind.

She practically had a heart attack as she jumped and screamed.

"What the fuck?" she yelled when she realised it was you grinning sheepishly. "Where the hell have you been? I haven't heard from you for days." And then immediately on the heels of that looking up in the air, confused, "Did you just fall from the sky?"

"I will answer all your questions," you promised as you kissed Vasia on the lips.

There was a knock at the door and with a defiant look, you added "I'll answer that. Stay here where it's safe."

"I don't understand," Vasia said as you retreated into the house. "What's going on? What do you mean, be safe?" She added all questions.

"I will explain everything later," you promised over your shoulder.

You reached the door, took the chain off and opened it wide to reveal the three balaclava-wearing men.

"I hear you're looking for me," you announced to the one with the rifle.

You didn't give the man a chance to react. You moved forward and punched him squarely in the jaw, and the man went flying.

Before the first even touched the floor, you moved onto the second guy. You punched him in the stomach, and as he was doubling over, you gave him an uppercut to the jaw too.

You pivoted around on your dominant foot and delivered a roundhouse kick against the side of the third guy's face.

All three men landed on the floor at practically the same time—all unconscious.

This all happened in a matter of seconds. You used your super-speed without even realising you were doing it.

You stood over the unconscious men surveying what you had done when you heard the recognisable sound of a car door opening and shutting from behind.

You turned and saw the fourth man standing by the side of the black Range Rover brandishing a stun gun.

Arrogantly thinking you would not get hurt, you confidently strode up to the guy, saying, "Now put that down, you don't want to get hurt."

The guy with the stun gun either didn't hear you or just didn't listen but with no word of warning he fired.

You saw that he would do this, and a smug smile crossed your face.

That smile quickly faded into a frozen contortion of pain as the small metal rods embedded in your chest and sent a million volts of electricity coursing through your body.

Once upon a time, you accidentally touched an electric fence when out hiking, and the feeling you got from that was unpleasant but didn't hurt so much as a tingle and only lasted for the second you had your hand on the fence.

This was much, much worse. You fell to the floor and started convulsing, writhing in pain like a fish out of water.

You were conscious throughout the entire thing. The pain seemed to go on forever. You were aware that you were going to lose control of my bladder and felt something warm spreading on your crotch.

You vaguely heard Vasia from behind, not paying any heed to your command earlier, coming to the door asking what was happening and then screaming as she saw you writhing about on the floor with a balaclava-wearing man standing over you with a stun gun.

After that, you weren't sure what was happening as you began slipping in and out of consciousness. What seemed like an eternity, your body suddenly stopped convulsing.

This was mainly because, after her initial scream, Vasia wasted no time in rushing the balaclava-wearing man and shoved him. He almost fell to the floor but regained his balance. However, he dropped the stun gun, putting an end to the electrical discharge.

As the effects of the electric shock wore off and you started feeling more like yourself. You looked up in time to see the man and Vasia in the middle of vicious hand to hand combat.

At one point the man rushed Vasia, but she swiftly moved out of the way and, using his momentum to help, she pushed him in the back. His face smashed the passenger window launching glass everywhere.

Upon hearing a commotion, some neighbours had come out of their houses. They were watching with that morbid fascination that nosy neighbours have.

When Vasia put the man's head through the car window, a couple of them involuntarily screamed before putting their hands over their mouths. One neighbour, an overweight middle-aged, balding man who was obviously a wrestling fan, yelled in congratulatory surprise and fist-pumped the air as if he was watching one of his TV shows.

Stunned, the balaclava man slid down the side of the car and onto the floor. On his back, he tried to get a knife out from his trouser pocket, but still groggy, Vasia simply kicked it away, and it disappeared down a drain.

For good measure, as the man tried to stand up, Vasia stooped down and punched the man squarely in the face, completely knocking him out.

With all four men now laying on the floor unconscious, Vasia helped you stand up.

"Are you ok?" she asked, concerned. And then a little less concerned, "Where the hell have you been?"

Still feeling unsteady you bravely answered "I'm ok. But I think I've found one of my weaknesses."

Not getting the reference Vasia looked at you quizzically. Noticing, you added, "I'll tell you inside," and then, looking down at yourself, embarrassed "I need to change."

*

Moments later, you had changed. As you were going to the London Marathon, the best thing you thought you could wear was your running gear, complete with a racing number pinned to your front,

"Great! You thought to yourself. *"I'm going to attempt to save the world in my blue and yellow trainers."*

You were telling Vasia an abridged version of what had happened to you since leaving her at Heathrow Airport.

When you mentioned the vision of the nuclear bomb exploding in London and that you aimed to stop it she understandably expressed concern.

"No, it's not safe" Like only a loving wife could say.

"Don't worry," you reassured Vasia. "I've got superpowers, remember."

"Yes, but from what I gather you're not completely indestructible, you can still get shot and die," Vasia said matter-of-factly.

"But I always come back," you quickly pointed out.

"And what of the stun gun? Huh, what about that?!"

You paused for a moment, as you didn't have an answer for that one. Eventually getting slightly defensive, you said, "Look! Who else do you think will stop this?"

"Gee, I don't know," Vasia answered sarcastically. "The police!"

You were just about to come out with some equal sarcastic comeback when, as if right on cue, there was a knock at the door.

"Now if that's the police I will scream," you muttered as you went to the front door and opened it.

And standing outside was the police! More precisely, it was Detective Stone and Special Agent Haider.

They were both watching the balaclava-wearing men as they groggily and sheepishly picked themselves up from the floor. After seeing the two detectives staring at them, they promptly got back in their car, without a word, and drove away.

As the Range Rover disappeared, Stone and Haider silently exchanged a knowing look before turning and noticing you were standing in the doorway.

"Mr Emerson," Stone started, efficiently, without so much as a hello. "Do you mind coming with us?"

228

Although it was phrased as a question, the way Stone emphasised it meant that you didn't really have any other choice but to go.

"Where to?"

"Back to the station at Scotland Yard," answered Stone, who looked a little confused with my question.

"We need you to answer some questions to help with our investigation," Haider added.

You didn't care for the way Haider emphasised the world "help", but you calmly shrugged your shoulders and said, "Fine, I'm going that way, anyway."

"Is everything ok?" a concerned Vasia asked from behind.

"Yes, these nice guys just want to have a chat with me," you responded, trying to sound reassuring as you turned to face Vasia.

"What about the you know what?" Vasia whispered so that Stone and Haider couldn't hear.

"It'll be fine, I promise," you whispered back and tenderly kissed Vasia on the lips. "Besides, you're probably right they might be able to help." You added before you stepped out of the door and closed it behind you.

*

For a few moments, Vasia stood facing the closed door watching you and the detectives walk away through the frosted glass. She was at a loss to say or do. The impending explosion in London was playing heavily on her mind. Flash backs to the underground not weeks before splashed like ice water on her face through her mind.

You wanting to save the world was bad. Being escorted by the police was somehow worse.

The day Ermee appeared in her car and what she told Vasia about what she could make of it all kept playing in her head as well.

Eventually, she concluded that she couldn't do anything and to ease her mind, she went into the living room, switched on the TV and tuned to BBC 1.

At the moment some cookery show was on, but in a while, they would start broadcasting from the marathon as the last preparations got underway before the big start.

Vasia sat down and kept her eyes on the TV with grim and avid interest.

Chapter 28

With the sirens on and Detective Stone driving at speed, it took forty-five minutes to zoom down the motorway and to Victoria Embankment in the centre of London where Scotland Yard HQ was based.

The journey, although speedy to the point of being dangerously vomit-inducing, it still felt like an excruciatingly long time with an uncomfortable silence all the way there. You tried to make small talk with the men but failed.

It wasn't until you went into the interview room at Scotland Yard that Stone and Haider spoke. The interview room was compact and square at about ten by ten foot with grey undecorated stone walls and was dimly lit by one naked strip light on the ceiling. The only furnishings were a grey wooden table and four chairs. It reminded you of old episodes of *The Bill.*

The Detective and Special Agent sat on one side of the table with you on your own facing them.

As you sat down, you spotted a basic, white, round analogue clock above the entrance to the interview room. You silently noted the time was now 8:15 am, an hour and forty-five minutes before the start of the London Marathon.

Haider noticed you looking at the clock. With a subtle tinge of sarcasm, he asked, "Do you have somewhere to be?" It was the first thing he had said to you since leaving the house.

Indicating the running number on your top, you answered truthfully, "I'm running in the London Marathon, it starts soon."

"That's great. Are you running for a charity?" Stone asked conversationally.

Slightly put off by Stone's sudden conversational tone, you stuttered a bit when you answered, "Yes, I'm running for Orchid, the male cancer charity."

"I know the one, they helped my dad when he had cancer," Stone said, looking thoughtful.

What followed was another uncomfortable silence that can only be caused when someone divulges something personal that's inappropriate for the situation they are in.

Haider, getting right down to serious business, broke the silence by getting his dictaphone out of his suit breast pocket and after switching it on he said "This is Special Agent Haider and Detective Stone interviewing Simon Emerson regarding the Green Park Terrorist Attack on March Sixteenth. It has been made clear to Mr Emerson that he has not been arrested. He has come willingly to answer questions and help with the police investigation."

You didn't know whether or not you were paranoid, but you didn't like the way Haider emphasised the phrase "help with the police investigation." It made you wonder what would happen if you accidentally gave the two detectives an answer they didn't like.

After Haider finished with the introduction, Stone said, "Now I know it's been two weeks and we have made you do this before but can you tell us, again, in your own words, the events that led up to the terrorist attack on Green Park Underground Station."

You recounted your previous statement from when you first saw the Green Hood to being knocked out by the explosion and being sent to hospital.

"Did you know this person in the green hood?" Haider asked suddenly.

"No," you said, confused by the question.

Stone passed over a piece of A4 paper. It was a screengrab of a CCTV image. You could clearly see yourself standing up in the tube train hanging onto a grab rail. There were other random people about but what caught your eye was the Green Hood standing right next to you. Seeing the terrorist standing so close but not actually able to remember it gave you the creeps.

"This picture shows The Green Hood standing next to you, and in the actual CCTV footage, we know it was for a considerable amount of time. Do you remember him?" Stone asked. There was a slightly accusatory tone underlying the question.

"No, I don't remember," you answered, trying not to sound defensive.

"Did you speak to him or did he speak to you?"

"No, he didn't."

"How do you know if you don't remember?"

"Because I would have remembered that."

"What about when he stepped off the train?"

"I shouted after him because I noticed he had left his bag."

"And he turned to you?"

"Yes."

"Did you see his face?"

"No, the hood completely covered it."

"Did he speak to you?"

"No. He just stood there."

You were getting increasingly uneasy by this barrage of questioning. You had the feeling that the Detective and Special Agent were trying to get you to slip up about something.

Unexpectedly the Detective and Special Agent suddenly abandoned the current line of questioning and started asking you about other things.

"You were in the hospital after the attack for a little while, weren't you?"

"Yeah for a day or two," you answered, trying to sound nonchalant.

"In fact, you were in a coma because you seriously injured your head."

"Yes," you agreed.

"You seem to have healed quite nicely."

"Yes,".

"Did you have any visitors while in the hospital?"

"Just my wife and dad," you answered truthfully.

"You also had a visit from two tourists from Africa?"

"Really?" You really didn't have a clue what the Detective was talking about for a moment. Then the other shoe dropped when you realised it must have been Ermee and Eraaf.

"Yes, while you were asleep."

"Oh."

"Do you know their names?"

"No, I was asleep," you answered, trying your best not to sound too sarcastic but failing.

This was your first lie to the police but, remembering that the Xuholos wanted to be kept a secret, you thought that was the best thing to do. Then as if it was some minor thing that you had just remembered you added, "But they must have been the granddaughter and grandfather that I helped rescue from the train."

"Yes, they must have been," Haider agreed but with a certain amount of animosity to show he wasn't impressed with the answer.

Haider then reached into a pocket on the inside of his suit pocket and produced a tablet. While he was doing something on it, he said, "Do you know the African man went into your room one night. Our working theory is that he did something to pull you out of your coma. Do you know what it was?"

"No, I didn't know." But you had a very good guess.

"Yes, we have got CCTV footage of the hallway outside your old room in the hospital," Haider said, handing the tablet to you.

You took it and watched the video that was playing on it. As Haider mentioned, it was the footage from a CCTV camera in the hospital's hallway, outside the room you had been in two weeks ago. It was black and white and was slightly fuzzy, but you could make out Eraaf walking up the hallway and into your room. The door closed and a moment later you could see a brilliant white light through the cracks of the door. Moments later, Eraaf exited the room and calmly walked back the way he had come.

Just before the door to your room closed, you could see your body convulsing on the bed. Shortly after Eraaf disappeared, a nurse came running into the room obviously alerted by some sound and could be seen shouting up the hallway.

"So that's how it happened." you thought to yourself. Uptil now, how you had woken up in hospital so quickly had always been a mystery to you.

Without saying a word, trying to act as casual as possible, you calmly handed the tablet back to Haider once the video had stopped.

"Do you want to explain that?" asked Haider, unnerved by your quietness.

"Sorry, explain what?" you asked, feigning confusion.

"Why did the African man in the video enter your room when you were asleep?"

"I don't know, I was asleep," you answered smartly.

"What about the light?"

"I have no idea," Which was not actually a lie. Although you have seen Eraaf's staff glow on a couple of occasions now you really didn't have any idea what it was. "I'm guessing it might have been a camera flash." You added before it occurred to you that if that explanation was ever true you should be worried.

"We reckon he pulled you out of a coma."

"What, you mean like a doctor?"

Haider paused and with a dangerous glint in his eye stared at me for a few moments. It took all your willpower not to look away from that stare.

Eventually, it was Stone who broke the silence this time. "What have you been up to since you have been out of the hospital?"

"Not much. Been recovering, looking for work, as I am out of a job."

"I remember you saying you were in London that day for an interview. Did you find out if you were successful?" Stone's tone seemed to be genuinely interested, but you had the feeling that he didn't actually care.

"No, they sent me one of those letters that said thank you for coming, but we regret to tell you you weren't successful blah, blah, blah."

"Sorry to hear that, I bet that disappointed you."

"It did," you said, feigning slight depression. "But life goes on as they say. Besides, I have another interview next week."

"Good luck with that."

You expressed your thanks, and then Stone abruptly changed the subject.

"Are you aware that there was a traffic accident on junction 11 of the M1 near your home, Friday last week?"

You paused for a moment not knowing how to respond. Then realising you had paused for too long and thinking that would look bad you tried to think of something quick. The result was that you purposefully pulled your face into a frown as if you were trying to remember something insignificant, "Yes, I think so, I think I remember hearing something on the news about some big pile up." you responded.

"Were you there at all?"

You were about to deny being there when you remembered all the people with smartphones videoing and taking pictures of you. A dreadful paranoid thought came when it suddenly occurred to you that the police could have cleared up the video and pictures or even got hold of clearer footage that the public didn't know about that could show you in clearer HD like quality.

"Oh you mean the car accident." You suddenly recalled. "Yes. I remember now," you added cautiously. "There was a lady and her baby I saved, and we got away from a truck before it exploded."

You may be able to lie but you were no *Gus Fring.*

Both Stone and Haider smirked at you, which made you realise that maybe you weren't paranoid after all.

"Really?" Haider said sceptically. "You got away?"

"Yes," you answered defiantly, trying hard to keep looking Haider in the eye.

Haider switched on the tablet again and navigated to another video.

He handed it back to you and said, "This is a video from a satellite that was passing over the area at the time of the accident."

With growing dread, you watched as the video offered a bird's-eye view of the motorway accident. It started from the moment you pulled the unconscious man from the Mini. Even though for most of the video you could only see the tops of people's heads, there was a brief flash of your face for a second when you were pulling the guy out of the car. You watched as you got the guy to safety and then there was the lady you helped. And then the explosion. The sudden brightness caused you to look away from the screen for a moment.

When you looked back, you could see the ball of fire receding to reveal someone, crouching on the floor. At first, you could only see the top of his back, which at first resembled a burnt smoking hog roast and then the dark charred parts began disappearing to reveal blemish-free skin.

You remembered the excruciating pain and a split second before the video showed it; you recalled you looked up while you were screaming. And there it was. The video stopped on the exact moment it showed your screaming face contorted in agonising pain, in glorious HD quality.

For a moment, you were afraid to look up. Trying not to look at the two officers you handed the tablet back to Haider.

"It's amazing what they can do with special effects these days isn't it." you finally uttered.

"Can you explain how you healed like that?" Haider asked, ignoring your comment.

"What do you mean?" you asked, feigning confusion again. "It's obviously a fake. You can't actually think I can heal that fast like that. I mean that's something straight out of a superhero comic book movie."

Both Stone and Haider gave you a look that you took to mean a variety of things:

1. That they didn't believe a word you were saying
2. That they knew you could heal super-fast was precisely what they were suggesting.
3. But they knew in reality that couldn't happen and didn't want to look the fools for saying it out loud.
4. No court in the land would believe them, anyway.

Instead, Stone changed the subject and said, "We know last Saturday you flew from Heathrow to Cairo and then got a connecting flight to Khartoum in Sudan. What were you doing there?"

"I was there on holiday?"

"Without your wife?" Haider asked, always sceptical

"Yes, it was a stag do," you answered, thinking on my feet.

"What was it? A holiday or stag do?"

"Err... Both."

"You're out of a job, and you paid for a holiday to Sudan?"

"I'm sure you already know, my wife gets paid very well, and we've got savings?" Which wasn't a lie.

"How did you get back? We don't have any records of you coming back into the country."

"I flew back," you responded, deciding it was best to keep to the truth. "Your records must be faulty."

Stone and Haider gave you that same skeptical look for a moment, and then Haider said, "You met a colleague of ours in Cairo."

"I did?"

"Yes, we had you followed, and our colleague said he saw you do some amazing things."

"Really? Like what?"

For a moment, you looked up at the clock and noted that it was now nine o'clock. An hour before the marathon was due to start. It occurred to you that if something drastic didn't happen, you were not getting out of here anytime soon.

"Yes," Stone was saying, "our colleague shot you on two separate occasions. Once in the chest and the second time in the head. Both times were fatal, but you somehow survived both shots."

"He must have missed."

"And then he said you tied him up."

"He was trying to follow and shoot me," you pointed out.

"So you admit you met our colleague?"

"Only because you said he followed and tried to kill me. You didn't say that before."

As I said before you're no *Gus Fring*.

"Luckily he got out of his restraints fairly quickly, and before he flew back to the UK, he found you again in the gym and took this video," Haider said.

He once again handed the tablet to you.

You took it with another sinking feeling in your stomach and watched the video playing on the tablet. This video was short and filmed through the glass windows of the doors leading into the gym. It was shaky, but you could make out yourself and Kosey, practising on the mats. It was the moment Kosey was pushing me to get a reaction, and then you shoved him, and he went flying down the other end of the gym. Kosey went out of view of the camera, but you could hear Kosey crashing into the treadmills like bowling pins.

Silently and looking less relaxed than before, you handed the tablet back to Haider. As you did so, you looked up at the clock again. It was now 9:05 am.

Stone seeing that you had looked at the clock again, unpleasantly asked, "Do you have somewhere to be?"

You took a cleansing breath.

"I told you before. I'm in the marathon. It starts in less than an hour."

"You're not going anywhere," Haider said confrontationally, suddenly raising his voice. "Not until you have explained all this to our satisfaction."

"Explained what?" you asked, getting agitated.

Haider started numbering the points on his fingers. "Explain what you were doing in London on the day of the attack? Explain how you healed so quickly from the attack? Explain what the African man was doing in your hospital room? Explain what happened at the motorway accident a week ago? Explain what you were doing in Sudan and how you got back when there are no records of you getting back? Explain how, despite being in the middle of an explosion and being fatally shot twice, you're still standing here with not so much as a scratch on you?" Haider stopped for a breather and Stone finished for him.

"And explain how you pushed a man twice your size across what looks like the entire length of that gym?"

240

What followed was an uncomfortable silence as you tried to think a way out of this. It didn't escape your notice that you were well and truly stuck between a rock and a hard place. Giving up, you finally said "Ok. I'll tell you everything, but you won't believe me."

"Try us."

Taking a deep breath, you proclaimed, "I have superpowers."

You don't know how you were expecting Stone and Haider to react. Maybe laugh or something. But all you got was stony faces. You felt a bit deflated.

Calmly, Stone asked "Tell us the whole story."

Conscious of the time, you gave them an abridged version of it, right from the train accident to now.

On hearing there would be another terrorist attack in London, Haider and Stone sat up to attention.

"When and where?" asked Stone, making it more of a command than a question.

"At ten o'clock outside Greenwich Observatory at the starting line of the London Marathon."

In unison Stone and Haider, both looked at the clock. It was now 9:30 am, thirty minutes before the start of the London Marathon.

Stone and Haider urgently stood up and walked out of the interview room.

"Hey? What about me? I can help," you said to their retreating backs.

"Stay here," Stone ordered, not bothering to turn around. He and Haider were out of the room and closed the door.

There was an audible click, meaning one thing. You got up from your seat and went over to try the door. After confirming that they had locked it, you cursed.

For a moment, you reluctantly resigned to the fact that you couldn't do anything but sit and wait.

However, after a very long ten minutes, you decided you had had enough. Time was running out.

"This is getting ridiculous." you said to yourself.

You stood up, walked to the door and with that now-familiar primordial power feeling growing inside you, you kicked the door open. It did more than open; it came totally off its hinges and flew into the wall opposite in a massive cacophony of noise.

You found yourself in a narrow white corridor lit by dim strip lights. Other doors led to other interview rooms.

You were not bothering to wait to see if anyone had heard the noise. You ran at super-speed down the hallway and out of the nearest exit.

Outside, you found yourself in a courtyard with a dozen or more police cars and vans parked up. Two police officers were talking down the far end of the yard, but they didn't notice you.

You were about to launch up into the sky when a thought came to you. You were learning that you couldn't just rush in and rescue people like you had been doing. You were putting your identity at risk. The Xuholos' identity at risk. You needed a disguise.

As if on cue, a motorbike courier rode into the courtyard and stopped by the exit you had just come out of. Dressed all in black leather and wearing a helmet with a shaded visor the courier switched off his engine as you walked up to him.

The courier took his helmet off to reveal a twenty-something Asian man with long bleached blond hair.

"I need your clothes, your boots and your helmet," you immediately demanded of the courier.

Not missing a beat, the courier, looked at you with some amusement, "Dude! You're meant to say you need my motorcycle too!"

Chapter 29

Minutes later at Greenwich Park over 40,000 excited runners were getting ready to run the London Marathon. Easily triple that number of spectators were equally happy to watch them go.

In the noisy party atmosphere, the Green Hood was walking through the crowds of laughing children and excited adults parallel to the runners.

Casually the Green Hood split off and started heading towards Greenwich Observatory.

He was nearing the park bench that he meant to put the bomb under when a person dressed all in black biker leathers and helmet seemingly dropped out of the sky and landed right in front of him.

The Green Hood stopped dead. You couldn't see his face, but you could tell he was taken by surprise. There were many people around, sitting on the grass or walking to join the rest of the marathon spectator. Some saw this and had to do a double-take.

Most carried on walking. A few stragglers who were more inclined to believe their eyes and could smell something was going to happen between this mysterious hooded figure, and flying biker carried on watching. Some even got their smartphones out, feeling the opportunity for some great selfies and videos.

Ignoring all the people around but leaving your shaded visor down, you shouted to the Green Hood, "Stop! You do not need to do this."

The Green Hood ignored your request and started moving towards you.

"I'm warning you. Stop!" You commanded again, with what you hoped was more force.

In one swift movement, The Green Hood pulled out a Japanese Katana sword from a hidden scabbard, behind his back and started expertly waving it around in wide intimidating arcs.

"Oh shit," You gulped. "Kosey did not teach me this."

The Green Hood rushed forward and brought his Katana down in a wide arc.

Even using your super-speed, you barely dodged the sword by stepping to the side.

You punched the Green Hood in the abdomen, but it hardly seemed to affect him.

The Green Hood brought his sword up and then down again for another swipe.

You dodged it again. Pivoting on your dominant leg, you delivered a perfect roundhouse kick to the Green Hood's chest.

The Green Hood stumbled and stepped back, but he recovered astonishingly fast allowing him to avoid a devastating uppercut.

He brought his sword down. This time he took you by surprise and you weren't lucky enough to dodge it in time. He sliced right through your arm, chopping it off. You fell to the floor in agony holding your bloody stump. The lower part of your arm fell to the ground next to you. With a sudden feeling of claustrophobia, you somehow ripped your bike helmet off with one hand. Now free from the confines, the ever-excruciating agony caused you to arch your back, and you let out a piercing scream towards the heavens.

The people around clasped their mouths in shock. A couple even vomited at the sight of blood squirting out of your stump. Some, however, just thought this was some show with hyper-realistic effects and carried on filming with their smartphones, none the wiser.

As you cradled your stump, The Green Hood turned and started towards the park bench again.

He only managed two steps. "Wait." you said.

He stopped and turned around when he heard you talking. You were holding your stump up in the air, but something was happening. It was gradually growing into an arm.

Although the Green Hood's face couldn't be seen, you could tell he was watching both stunned and captivated.

The people who had vomited now fainted. The others who were filming or had stronger constitutions gave a loud cheer.

Just as four new fingers and one thumb appeared, you stood up and rushed towards The Green Hood.

The Green Hood turned to make a run, but you caught him and grabbed him from behind. Holding onto the Green Hood with a vice-like grip, you pulled the hood down and gasped in confusion and surprise.

Taking advantage of your shock, The Green Hood broke out of your grip and turned to face you with an evil smirk on her face.

He was a woman! You estimate she was in her thirties, athletic looking as if she may be a wrestler or some Amazonian warrior. Her face was harsh with a gaunt, pale complexion and long blond hair tied in a tight ponytail. Her blue eyes had a harsh cold aspect to them as she stood there smirking at you.

You went to grab her again, but you had hesitated too long. The Green Hood took advantage and disappeared. And when I say she disappeared, she literally vanished. With an undramatic pop.

Stupefied, All you could do was stand there wondering where the woman had gone.

The crowd also wondered where the woman had gone to. Even the ones videoing the scene had to look up from their smartphones to confirm with their eyes that she was no longer there.

At that moment, a quick vision came to you, and you stepped to the side. Just in time as you saw a Katana blade stab the empty space where your body would have been seconds before.

You swiveled around and caught hold of The Green Hood's sword-wielding fist just as she was bringing it back down.

You tapped her in the nose with her own fist. Her nose bloodied. What caught you off guard next was that the broken nose healed.

Arriving at the comprehension that she can heal like you, you declared "Well, that's just fantastic. We're just going to carry on like this all day?"

Not bothering to answer you she head-butted you. You staggered back letting go of her arm. You recovered in time to avoid the next Katana swing, and you ducked as she tried to bring it round to cut your head off.

On her third try, you grabbed her Katana wielding wrist again, turned, lifted her over your shoulders and down again onto her back. Still holding the Green Hood's wrist, you twisted it and knocked the Katana out of her hand.

Staring up at you with a degree of hatred that was enough to melt your face off, she vanished again.

Leaving no time for you to react, she reappeared. This time standing up, right in front of you. She delivered a left and then a right jab to your abdomen and vanished again.

She reappeared behind. She planted her foot against your bottom and pushed you to the floor where you got a face full of grass.

The Katana had fallen out of your hand, and The Green Hood stooped down to retrieve it. As she picked it up, you grabbed hold of her nearest foot squeezed and pulled.

She fell on her back and in one movement, you jumped back up. You stood over her as you demanded. "You need to stop. I can't let you kill all these people."

Wordlessly, smirking with those cold blue eyes of hers that never left yours she stood up.

Sensing what would happen next, you went to grab the Green Hood. Before, you could get to her though she vanished again.

A nano-second later she reappeared and delivered a roundhouse kick to your face. You staggered, and she disappeared again.

Before you could recover, she reappeared and disappeared in quick succession. Before she vanished, she planted an uppercut to your chin. You lost your balance and started to fall.

You were still falling when she reappeared from behind, and karate kicked you in the neck. She vanished again.

She reappeared in mid-air above you. You were ready for her this time, though. You grabbed hold of her before she could disappear.

This time she took you with her.

You landed on your back on something hard with a massive "Ommmpphhh" as The Green Hood landed on top of you.

For a moment, your noses almost touched. You could smell her furious breath against your face. It vaguely reminded you of lavender.

If anyone was around to witness, they would think you were in a compromising situation.

In a hurry you both stood up you squared off again.

It took you a few moments to realise you were no longer at Greenwich Park. Momentarily confused, you looked around. You were standing in a back alley of some sort, with a cobblestone floor and brick walls smudged with centuries of grime towering above you. You breathed a sigh of relief when you realised we were still in London. At one end of the alleyway in not so far away distance, you could see the London Eye.

Taking advantage of your confusion, The Green Hood went to stab you with her Katana.

A vision momentarily warned you this would happen. You quickly shook off your confusion. You grabbed the lady's arm just before she could plunge her sword into you. The tip was only millimetres away from your chest.

Like you did before you used her fist to punch her in the face.

In quick succession, you gave her an uppercut to the jaw and then a jab to the abdomen. Before she could recover, you pivoted and landed a roundhouse kick. She went headfirst into a brick wall with a satisfying thump sound.

Rubbing the back of her head, the lady looked more annoyed than hurt. She went into a fight pose, but then it seemed like a bright idea crossed her mind.

She looked up the alleyway towards the London Eye and you followed her gaze. She looked back at you and gave you a cheeky wave before she vanished.

"Oh, no, you don't" you muttered conscious of where she was going.

Blue sparks of electrical swirls surrounded you and you launched off at super-speed. You ran down the alleyway, across busy roads, avoiding everyone who was about.

You climbed over a red double decker bus and squeezed in between two black London taxi cabs. One of the cab drivers was reading a newspaper and drinking builders tea out of a Styrofoam cup noticed when you sped past. The downdraft caused him to spill his hot tea over his lap. "That merchant is a real Barney Rubble." He muttered.

You went through a walkthrough tunnel. You found you had to run against the sides and ceiling to avoid pedestrians.

You came to the side of the Thames. Not missing a beat, you leaped across it. There was a party boat sailing past at the time and with one leg you landed on the roof. You rebounded off it and landed on the other side of the roof. You didn't stop or look back to see the one person who had seen you. An early twenty something female party goer who had a few too many drinks. For a moment she stared after you mouth agape. Looking at her cocktail glass she gingerly put it back down on the bar. "I have drunk way too much." She decided.

Within moments you were back at Greenwich Park. You saw the Green Hood ahead in the middle of the crowd who were still photographing and videoing. She had picked up the backpack and was on her way to putting it under the bench.

She had only got a few steps when she turned and saw you coming. Even with you super speed, The Green Hood still had exceptionally quick reflexes.

Just before you arrived like the bloody roadrunner, she vanished again.

You didn't have long to wonder where the woman had gone.

You instantly felt a stabbing pain in your back that carried on throughout your body until you witnessed the other end of the Katana breaking out through your stomach. The thought "I've been stabbed in the back," bearly registered in your mind before everything went black.

More of the public screamed and vomited. It shocked even the people videoing it all.

The Green Hood pulled out her sword from your body as you crumpled to the floor.

Checking that you were dead first she casually stepped over your body and carried on towards her destination. She didn't bother to wipe your blood of her sword.

As she went, she started fiddling with the buttons on the bomb inside the bag.

Nearing the park bench, she heard a noise behind her and turned around to see that you were standing right there.

The Green Hood tilted her head and allowed herself a smirk of surprise.

Just then Stone and Haider with a dozen armed police officers appeared from the crowd of spectators with guns drawn.

"Put that bag down!" Stone shouted with his gun aimed at the Green Hood.

However, the Green Hood was not about to pay any attention to any demands. She whistled to you. The first time you noticed any sound coming out of her mouth.

You looked round in time to see her throwing you the backpack. You caught it with comic awkwardness.

With everyone's attention temporarily on the bag, the Green Hood did her disappearing trick and vanished. Permanently this time.

In the not so far distance you vaguely heard the announcer for the London Marathon was telling everyone the marathon was about to start in sixty seconds.

Looking down in the bag, the timer was also counting down from sixty seconds.

In a flash, you looked up at the spectators and the newly arrived police officers who all now had their guns aimed at you.

"I'm warning you, put the bag down!" Stone shouted again.

"Err, I can't do that," you responded, on the verge of panicking.

For the moment, you had no idea what to do, and you were genuinely bricking it. You looked around at the faces in the crowd which had formed around the police officers and you.

You looked further on at the spectators for the marathon and the runners getting ready to run.

"Fifty seconds," the announcer said.

"One last warning, I will not tell you again. Drop the bag," Stone shouted.

You were very aware that all these people would be dead soon if you didn't do something.

Your gaze fell on the nearest person filming you. A teenage boy with his smartphone.

A random thought popped into your head when you understood that your identity was now well and truly comprised.

"I will be famous."

"Forty-five seconds," the announcer said.

Promptly deciding, a look of grim determination spread across your face as you slipped the backpack on.

"Film this," you dared the teenage boy.

Without warning, you shot up into the sky. You caused a downdraft that almost knocked the spectators and police off their feet.

Caught by surprise, they all cursed and looked up after your fast disappearing form.

Stone, Haider and the armed police officers were now feeling a little impotent with their guns now trained on thin air.

Looking up at your fast disappearing form with awe, Stone said, "That's not something you see every day."

"Yeah, everything he said in the interview was true," Haider responded, equally dumbstruck.

"Imagine that."

Chapter 30

You weren't sure how high you had to go to protect everybody on the ground from the impending explosion from the nuclear bomb currently strapped to your back. You were no scientist, but what hundreds of action movies told you the higher, the better.

So, with a determined effort, you flew vertically straight up with your eyes on the heavens.

"Thirty-five seconds," the announcer announced.

You didn't hear this, you were already five miles up and flying through the clouds.

The air was getting thinner, and the temperature was getting colder, but you didn't feel it. You carried on through the troposphere and into the stratosphere.

Here the air was frigid. It was approximately minus fifty-three degrees Celsius. Ice started forming on your face, on your eyelids and in your hair.

The ozone here was so high that the air itself was toxic to a normal human being and at any rate, was too thin to breathe normally. This small minor fact still didn't affect you. Through gritted teeth, you ascended higher and higher and broke through to the mesosphere.

"Twenty-five seconds."

Here it was approximately minus one-hundred-and-one degrees Celsius. This was where aurorae such as the Northern Lights were formed, but still, the cold and lack of air didn't seem to show any effect on you.

It was getting darker and darker as you ascended further into the mesosphere and broke through to the thermosphere. You were now in the cold black darkness of space.

"Fifteen seconds."

You stopped and hovered above the Earth as it slowly rotated below you. The International Space Station flew by above. The sun was behind, and you could see the moon peeking from behind the Earth.

Further in the distance, you could just make out the red planet Mars. Other different systems and galaxies could be made out as well.

The sheer absurdity of being in space and being able to see all these wondrous sights were not lost on you. Or for the blindingly obvious that you were breathing.

You didn't have time to process all this though. You slipped the backpack off and peeked inside. The timer had just gone past ten seconds.

For a moment, you were unsure of what to do. Now that you were at a safe distance away from all the people on the ground, what were you going to do with the bomb now?

Conscious of the time, you arrived at a decision. With an overarm throw as if you were playing a game of cricket, you launched the bag further into space.

Wasting no time, you turned tail and flew back down to Earth.

Back on the ground, the London Marathon announcer was counting down the last five seconds till the start of the marathon. "Five... four... three..."

As you re-entered Earth's atmosphere, you were flying so fast that the friction with the ozone layer was causing your body to glow. Any faster and you would simply burn up.

"Two... one... zero."

Back on the ground, the klaxon sounded to start the London Marathon, and 40,000 excited runners proceeded to run. Although the ones at the back would have to wait a few minutes for the ones in front to move before they could start.

In the icy darkness of space, the bomb exploded in a brilliant bright flash of light and radiation.

Space is essentially a vacuum, so there was no sound, but EMP waves travel faster than normal. The first wave of radiation reached you quicker than you expected, and it enveloped you.

Feeling intense mind-numbing pain as your whole body began to turn into a black boiling husk, you screamed in pain and torment.

Your whole body was burning up. You were fighting to keep conscious. You would have likely evaporated away if it wasn't for the second massive EMP wave that struck and knocked into you propelling you forward, faster.

There was a moment where you remember thinking this is what it's like being in a head-on collision in a car and then nothing. Your world went black.

*

Hours later, Vasia was still where she had been that morning after you had left with the two detectives. Apart from getting a bite to eat and when she had to relieve herself, she had been religiously watching the marathon nonstop. She was avidly and nervously looking for a sign from you but saw nothing.

It concerned her, but the fact that there was no nuclear explosion was a big plus. So, she took comfort in that.

Towards the end of the marathon, after many thousands of runners had passed the finishing line, the ongoing commentary jumped to the news.

The usual handsome and dignified Huw Edwards was sitting at the news desk.

In his melodious Welsh tone he started "As we celebrate another fantastic year for the London Marathon, we see new records broken, personal bests beaten, a record turnout for runners and spectators alike. We know there will be stories to be told for years to come, but there is probably one story that has sparked the interest of thousands of people, and it has nothing to do with the Marathon itself. Jon Kay reports."

The screen flashed to the journalist Jon Kay who was standing in Greenwich Park with the observatory in the background

"Thank you, Huw," he said. "Now, with all eyes on the London Marathon today, you would have been forgiven for thinking that was the only thing going on here. However, some people have reported seeing something extraordinary.

We have footage to show you in a bit, but witnesses say they saw two people fighting, one of them described as a woman in her thirties with blonde hair wearing a green hoodie and carrying a Japanese Katana sword. The other was a man, also in his thirties, wearing biker leathers. The man was unarmed and seemed to be trying to prevent the woman from doing something.

Now this will sound crazy, but witnesses say that the man was stabbed fatally with the sword and even had an arm chopped off, but the arm grew back, and despite looking like he died he stood back up."

Immediately alert, Vasia sat forward in her chair.

"Then the police came, guns drawn, the woman seemed to disappear into thin air and then the man. And this is the crazy part, flew up into the sky carrying a backpack. He disappeared, but just over half a minute later, there was a ball of brilliant light in the sky. What was this? Was it some fantastic amateur dramatics show? Was it a new superhero Hollywood movie being filmed? Or did we just witness a real-life hero saving us from something that we can't quite comprehend yet? I'll let you judge for yourselves. Here's some mobile phone footage from the scene. I warn you though it can be a bit graphic."

Jon Kay's face disappeared, and in his place was a video. As it was from a mobile phone, the film was very amateur and shaky but Vasia could tell it showed what Jon Kay had just described.

She screamed with you when you had your arm chopped off. Then yelled in triumph when it grew back again.

"Huh, nobody saw that coming." She muttered to herself when it turned out the Green Hood was a blond-haired woman resembling an Amazonian warrior.

With the lousy camera phone graphics, she found it hard to keep track of the lady disappearing and reappearing repeatedly. Then you seemingly vanished with her.

Now, like the crowd on the television, she was wondering where the two of you had gone too.

Didn't have long to wait though. Within moments The Green Hood reappeared. She picked up the backpack and walked. She had only got two paces when as if on instinct, she looked around.

The next three things happened quickly, almost instantaneous.

The Green Hood disappeared.

You showed up.

The Green Hood reappeared and...

Vasia wanted to vomit after seeing the sword pierce your back and run through his chest. Seeing you on the floor, tears started rolling down her face, and then she shouted "YES" in triumph when you got back up.

Then the police showed up. The audio was lousy, but Vasia could make out Stone shouting at you to drop the bag that he was now holding. She could also hear the announcer for the London Marathon counting down the start of it.

You looked into the bag and seemed to think about something. Eventually, you looked straight into the mobile phone camera that was videoing you. The person on the other end of the phone for some inexplicable reason zoomed in on your face as if they were expecting something dramatic.

It occurred to Vasia that you would definitely need a disguise now.

She could hear you saying "Film this", and then he shot up into the sky. There was a scream of surprise from the crowd of spectators and the person videoing clumsily and shakily tried to track you.

The video kept rolling even long after you disappeared from view. There were roughly thirty seconds of blue sky when suddenly, a brilliant bright ball of light appeared.

There was a murmur of awe from the crowd of spectators as they had to shield their eyes from the initial sudden brightness. There were the beginnings of an orange and green auroral display that would last for several minutes.

Knowing what this all meant Vasia was now standing in front of the TV wishing to see you appear again.

"Come on, where are you?" She kept saying to herself.

You didn't quite appear on screen again, but there was another murmur from the crowd as the video showed a black dot in the distance falling fast and seemingly uncontrollable from the sky. It eventually disappeared behind some trees in the direction of Clapham Common.

The video stopped, and the image switched back to Jon Kay, who was saying,

"As you can see, something wonderful and strange happened here but was it real or some elaborate fake? Who were this hooded woman and biker? Where are they now? Did the biker just save us from something terrible? We asked to talk to the police, but they declined to comment. Now we have some information about what that black dot falling from the sky could have been. The following is a video of an eyewitness report from a dog walker at Clapham Common taken earlier today."

The screen switched to an elderly lady with wispy white hair carrying a Jack Russell under one arm. She seemed to be very self-conscious that she was on television. She was explaining what happened when she was out walking her dog earlier.

"I heard this loud thud, and this enormous crater just appeared in the middle of the common. I went to have a look and saw a naked man lying unconscious in it. I was shocked because it looked like he fell from the sky.

I wasn't looking for long when a big black Transit van came driving over to the common at speed and stopped by the crater. The back doors opened and out jumped these three big brutes all in balaclavas and carrying guns.

They rudely pushed me aside, went into the crater and carried the unconscious man out and dumped him in the van. Then they were gone."

The elderly woman's account finished, the screen switched back to Jon Kay.

"As I have said before." He started. "Wonderful and strange things have happened, and all we have are questions. Back to you, Huw."

The screen switched back to Huw in the newsroom, but Vasia was no longer paying attention to it as her mobile phone was ringing.

She looked at the caller display and noticed that it was Ron. Your Dad. With dreadful knowing and not relishing the imminent conversation, she reluctantly answered the phone.

"Hello, Ron," she said, trying to sound calm.

"Vasia, are you watching the news?" Ron sounded urgent.

"Yes."

"Was that him? Was that Simon?"

"Yes, Ron, it was him."

"Oh, my god. Where is he now?"

Realising that she had no idea where you were now, panic settled in, and it must have been evident in the sound of her voice. "No, I don't know where he is, I haven't seen him since this morning."

"Ok, I'm coming, I will get the next train."

Not bothering to wait for her response, Ron hung up, presumably to get ready to get the next train as promised.

Vasia put her phone down on the arm of the sofa, suddenly feeling very alone.

Her phone beeped, and she saw she had a text message from Zack, asking the same thing Ron had asked.

Her phone beeped a second time. It was a text message from her parents.

Her phone beeped a third time and then a fourth before it started uncontrollably.

Looking at the TV but not particularly paying any attention to it, tears came to her eyes and started rolling down her cheeks. She whispered in a small voice "Where are you, Simon?"

Chapter 31

You took in a deep breath and opened your chestnut brown eyes.

Confused and disorientated, it took you a few moments to notice your surroundings and your current predicament. You were tied crucifix style, to a grey breeze block wall with chains.

You tried to struggle out of the chains, but all your strength had left you. You quickly gave up.

You surveyed the concrete room you were in. Dimly lit by one fluorescent strip, the only furnishing was a simple wooden table in the far corner. On top of the table, there were various grim-looking instruments—a steak knife, a machete, an assault rifle, and what looked like dynamite.

The only other thing in the room was a vast landscape mirror opposite you.

You noticed you were wearing nothing but a white hospital gown and was not pleased about it. You saw a shadow move behind the mirror, and realised it was a one-way window.

"Hello," you called in a hoarse voice that you did not recognise. "Is anyone there?"

A moment later, the door to the room opened and in walked a tall person in black combat gear and wearing a balaclava over his face.

"Hey mate, let me out of this." He ignored you, "Hello? The least you can do is tell me where I am." Without a word, he crossed the room to the table.

He looked down and picked up the steak knife. Your stomach sank. Before turning back to you, he threw a cursory glance into the window mirror.

You noticed above the one-way window, a speaker. As if on cue, a deep male voice came through on a speaker. "Proceed with test one," it said.

"What's test one?" you asked, getting increasingly anxious as the man advanced on you.

The man stopped inches away from your face. You could smell the dinner he had just had on his brief. You guess it was spaghetti bolognaise.

It was easy to understand what this man was going to do. Panic started boiling inside you.

You started begging the man, "Uh hey, you want to reconsider what you're gonna do? I'd really appreciate it."

Showing no emotion, the man plunged the steak knife all the way to the hilt into your chest just where your heart was. For a moment, the coldness of the blade going in was accentuated by the coppery taste on your tongue. You didn't have time to process the pain. you instantly died.

*

"I remember now." I say to the bearded man.

"Good." The man answers

"No." I shake my head sadly. "I remember everything. I remember how they have tortured me non stop and how it hurts so much. I don't know how long I have been here, I have lost track.

"You've been here for two weeks." The man confirms "But I am here to get you out."

"How?" I look at the man.

There are tears in my eyes. The last couple of weeks of brutality and torture has made me a broken man.

"I can't get out of here. They just keep killing me over and over again. My superpowers are useless here" And then something has just occurred to me. "I don't even know your name."

The man stands up and offers a hand to help me up. "My name is Arthur. When you went missing Kosey and the Xuholos asked me to look for you."

Reluctantly I take his hand and once we're face to face the man adds "Death can be a superpower too, and I can teach you how to control it."

TO BE CONTINUED...

Made in the USA
Las Vegas, NV
28 June 2021